A WALK IN MY WORLD

International Short Stories About Youth

EDITED BY ANNE MAZER

"Each of the sixteen stories in this compelling collection has a young person at its center. . . . Not only does this collection sweep around the globe, it compasses the human heart. The stories treat themes of enduring interest to youth. They are stories about growing up."

—Susan Marie Swanson, *Riverbank Review*

"These short stories highlight how different, and sometimes even how similar, the lives of young people are no matter where in the world they live. . . . a uniquely international short story collection, written by a distinguished group of authors. . . . "
—*VOYA*

" . . . high in literary merit and accessible to teens. . . . Mazer invites readers to examine and ponder pearls of wisdom collected from the intimate corners of six continents—and they will likely want to embark on future expeditions with the writers they encounter here."

—*Publishers Weekly* (starred)

"The theme is broad, but readers can dip into this global anthology one story at a time. The fine selections will also introduce teens to sixteen distinguished writers. . . . Teachers might like to use individual stories in cross-curriculum studies or as read-alouds to share."   —*Booklist*

" . . . offers many compelling tales for pleasure reading. . . . "
—*School Library Journal*

"[An] excellent compilation of short stories by internationally acclaimed authors. . . . "   —*MultiCultural Review*

OTHER PERSEA ANTHOLOGIES

America Street
A Multicultural Anthology of Short Stories
Edited by Anne Mazer

Going Where I'm Coming From
Memoirs of American Youth
Edited by Anne Mazer

Working Days
Short Stories About Teenagers at Work
Edited by Anne Mazer

Into the Widening World
International Coming-of-Age Stories
Edited by John Loughery

First Sightings
Contemporary Stories of American Youth
Edited by John Loughery

Paper Dance
55 Latino Poets
Edited by Victor Hernández Cruz, Leroy V. Quintana,
and Virgil Suarez

Show Me a Hero
Great Contemporary Stories About Sports
Edited by Jeanne Schinto

Virtually Now
Stories of Science, Technology, and the Future
Edited by Jeanne Schinto

A WALK IN MY WORLD

INTERNATIONAL

SHORT STORIES ABOUT

YOUTH

Edited, with an introduction by Anne Mazer

A KAREN AND MICHAEL BRAZILLER BOOK

PERSEA / NEW YORK

ACKNOWLEDGMENTS

I am grateful to Cornell University, which allowed me, as a local resident, to read in its outstanding collection, without which I would not have been able to complete this volume Thanks also to the Alternatives Library at Annabel Taylor Hall on the Cornell campus, and to Judy Busch, Karen Braziller, and Mark Braziller (age 13), who suggested the title   —A M

For information, write to the publisher:
Persea Books
277 Broadway, Suite 708
New York, NY 10007

Library of Congress Cataloging-in-Publication Data

A walk in my world : international short stories about youth / edited with an introduction by Anne Mazer.
p   cm.
"A Karen and Michael Braziller Book."
Summary: A collection of short stories from around the world including such authors as Valentin Rasputin, Yasunari Kawabata, and Toni Cade Bambara.
ISBN 0-89255-237-9 (alk. paper)
1 Children's stories [1 Short stories] I. Mazer, Anne.
PZ5 W13   1998
[Fic]—dc21   98-27861
                                                                                    CIP
                                                                                     AC

Designed by Leah Lococo
Typeset in Century, Copperplate, and Fling
by Keystrokes, Lenox, Massachusetts
Printed on acid-free, recycled paper, and bound
by The Haddon Craftsmen, Pennsyslvania.

5 6 7 8 9 10 11

CONTENTS

INTRODUCTION

Y ou are invited to a feast of stories, to stroll through a festival of the world's fiction. In this book you will find stories about twentieth-century youth written by some of the world's best writers. They come from every part of the globe and will take you to India for a game of hide-and-seek, on an errand in Cairo, to the arranged wedding of an eight-year-old girl in Indonesia, and on a walk through an Antiguan village that ends in a voyage overseas. You'll also meet young people in England, Ireland, Australia, Italy, Ghana, Germany, Norway, China, Japan, Chile, the United States, and Russia. Some of them are heroes for a cause; others are doing what they must to achieve their own independence. You'll recognize them because they are like you or someone you know. Yet they come from other cultures and speak other languages, and their lives are suffused with traditions that may extend back thousands of years. We invite you to take a walk in their world.

In the opening story, "The Jay," by Yasunari Kawabata, Yoshiko discovers a mother jay searching for its lost chick. Watching it, she is flooded with memories of her abandonment by her mother and a separation from her stepmother. When she helps the jay and chick find each other, she opens up the possibility of reconciliation in her own life. In "The Ladder" by V. S. Pritchett, divorce and stepmothers are viewed from a different perspective, as a fifteen-year-old girl, home from boarding school, becomes allies with her father against her new stepmother.

There are other kinds of families—and family problems—
in *A Walk in My World*. Yaaba, the heroine of Ama Ata Aidoo's
"The Late Bud," desperately wants to win her mother's love
although she cannot behave the way her mother wants her to.
The more she tries, the more she angers her mother. In some
cultures, families solve problems on their own; in this story
and culture, the whole village comes in to help. Frank
O'Connor's "Christmas Morning" is about the rivalry between
two brothers; one is studious, the other has no use for education. In "A Gentleman's Agreement" by Elizabeth Jolley, a family finds a way to leave the city and live on the land their grandfather has left them.

Play and games are the essence of childhood, and in
"Games at Twilight" by Anita Desai, a group of Indian children
slips out to their garden to play hide-and-seek on a scorching
afternoon. Ravi thinks he's outwitted his brothers and sisters
by hiding the longest, but when he triumphantly emerges from
his hiding place, he makes a shattering discovery. Naguib
Mahfouz's "The Conjurer Made Off with the Dish" begins as a
mother sends her son out for a plate of beans, which he never
brings home. Instead he gets distracted from his errand and
wanders into a series of mysterious encounters with a magician, a young girl, and a pair of lovers. Zeffirino, a young Italian
boy who is playing in the sea, also has an unusual encounter—
with a crying woman who won't be consoled—in Italo
Calvino's "Big Fish, Little Fish." In Cora Sandel's "The Child
Who Loved Roads," the girl likes to run down empty roads
because they make her feel alive and free, unlike the world of
adults, who let "everything truly fun [disappear] from their
lives . . ."

While the protagonist of Cora Sandel's story does not want
to abandon the joyful freedom of her play, Annie John, the nar-
rator of Jamaica Kincaid's story "A Walk to The Jetty," is ready

to cast off a once-beloved childhood world, which now feels too small for her. Her classmates get married and stay on, but Annie John has chosen to cross the ocean, become an immigrant, and go alone into a new culture. As she stands on the jetty, saying goodbye to her parents and preparing to leave her Antiguan village for England, she feels "a great gladness" but also as though "someone was tearing [her] up into little pieces . . ."

Toni Cade Bambara's "Sweet Town" is also about an adolescent girl's rite of passage, from a very different point of view. Fifteen-year-old Kit is devastated by the desertion of her two best buddies, her boyfriend B. J. and his sidekick Eddie, with whom she has just passed an exhilarating summer in New York City. The only way she can triumph over this disillusionment is by using the power of her imagination.

In some stories in *A Walk in My World*, the circumstances of young people's lives are unusually hard. Two stories, one from China and the other from Russia, take place in a school setting and have poor children at their center. "French Lessons," an autobiographical story by Valentin Rasputin, is set in the dire poverty of post-Second World War Siberia, when the communal farms of Communist Russia supplanted a thousand-year-old traditional way of life. In this story, a fifth-grade boy is sent away from his village to attend school in a larger town, where he struggles to keep alive on meager supplies of bread and potatoes that are stolen as soon as he receives them. In "Hands" by Xiao Hong, a poor girl from a family of dyers is also sent away at great sacrifice by her family to a boarding school where she is out of place and mercilessly taunted by the wealthier girls. Both the Russian boy and the Chinese girl struggle against difficult circumstances; both are determined to succeed against the odds; but one has a chance and the other doesn't. Wang Yaming is isolated and rejected by teachers and students alike, while the Russian boy is helped to survive by a sympathetic French teacher. Wang Yaming feels shame because she has failed her family; the boy is able to maintain his pride and sense of humor. Differing cultural and social conditions help determine their fates: the boy comes from the same social class as the other students and has had an equal education, while Wang Yaming is less educated and trying to better herself and her family in a society that looks down on her.

Freedoms also differ from country to country. Many of us take our freedoms for granted, but they are not the same everywhere in the world. Two stories show boys making decisions that have life-and-death consequences, while another unforgettably portrays the ill treatment girls receive in some cultures today. Pedro, a young Chilean boy in "The Composition" by Antonio Skármeta, is confused and frightened when the military police show up and take a friend's father away during a soccer game. The next day in school, while he is still trying to understand what has happened, he receives a seemingly harmless essay assignment that turns him and his friends into potential informers against their parents. In "The Balek Scales" by Heinrich Böll, a twelve-year-old boy discovers that his village has been cheated for decades by the rich family who buys their mushrooms, and he takes action to gain justice. "Inem," by Pramoedya Ananta Toer, recounts the fate of a very young girl married off by her family for money. Eight-year-old Inem tries to live with her seventeen-year-old husband, and then, when all her attempts have failed, to escape from him. Her dignity and courage—and, at the end, her utter abandonment by family and society—will move you.

Whether their circumstances are ordinary or extraordinary, the young people in *A Walk in My World* are all trying to make their way. They are sometimes confused and afraid, but they are also courageous and insightful; they sometimes struggle and hesitate, but they also make decisions and take action.

Their stories are compelling, realistic, and moving. Although *A Walk in My World* takes place in the twentieth century, our aim was not to mirror current events, which are always changing. Instead we have fashioned a collection of classic stories. Their authors are some of the most distinguished of the century: three Nobel Prize winners (Mahfouz, Böll, and Kawabata); many recipients of prestigious literary awards (Aidoo, Desai, Calvino, Skármeta, Kincaid, Jolley, Toer, Rasputin), two acknowledged twentieth-century masters of the short story in English (Pritchett, O'Connor), and several writers whose commitment to truth has led to their works being censored or banned in their own countries (Böll, Toer, O'Connor, Mahfouz). The stories were chosen with care from among hundreds of others, selected not only for their literary excellence but also to take you into the heart of another culture. We hope that you will be enriched by your sojourn there.

—ANNE MAZER

A WALK IN MY WORLD

THE JAY

Yasunari Kawabata

JAPAN

Since daybreak, the jay had been singing noisily.
When they'd slid open the rain shutters, it had flown up
before their eyes from a lower branch of the pine, but it
seemed to have come back. During breakfast, there was the
sound of whirring wings.

"That bird's a nuisance." The younger brother started to
get to his feet.

"It's all right. It's all right." The grandmother stopped him.
"It's looking for its child. Apparently the chick fell out of the
nest yesterday. It was flying around until late in the evening.
Doesn't she know where it is? But what a good mother. This
morning she came right back to look."

"Grandmother understands well," Yoshiko said.

Her grandmother's eyes were bad. Aside from a bout with
nephritis about ten years ago, she had never been ill in her life.
But, because of her cataracts, which she'd had since girlhood,
she could only see dimly out of her left eye. One had to hand
her the rice bowl and the chopsticks. Although she could grope
her way around the familiar interior of the house, she could not
go into the garden by herself.

Sometimes, standing or sitting in front of the sliding-glass door, she would spread out her hands, fanning out her fingers against the sunlight that came through the glass, and gaze out. She was concentrating all the life that was left to her into that many-angled gaze.

At such times, Yoshiko was frightened by her grandmother. Though she wanted to call out to her from behind, she would furtively steal away.

This nearly blind grandmother, simply from having heard the jay's voice, spoke as if she had seen everything. Yoshiko was filled with wonder.

When, clearing away the breakfast things, Yoshiko went into the kitchen, the jay was singing from the roof of the neighbor's house.

In the back garden, there was a chestnut tree and two or three persimmon trees. When she looked at the trees, she saw that a light rain was falling. It was the sort of rain that you could not tell was falling unless you saw it against the dense foliage.

The jay, shifting its perch to the chestnut tree, then flying low and skimming the ground, returned again to its branch, singing all the while.

The mother bird could not fly away. Was it because her chick was somewhere around there?

Worrying about it, Yoshiko went to her room. She had to get herself ready before the morning was over.

In the afternoon, her father and mother were coming with the mother of Yoshiko's fiancé.

Sitting at her mirror, Yoshiko glanced at the white stars under her fingernails. It was said that, when stars came out under your nails, it was a sign that you would receive something, but Yoshiko remembered having read in the newspaper that it meant a deficiency of vitamin C or something. The job of putting on her makeup went fairly pleasantly. Her eyebrows and lips all became unbearably winsome. Her kimono, too, went on easily.

She'd thought of waiting for her mother to come and help with her clothes, but it was better to dress by herself, she decided.

Her father lived away from them. This was her second mother.

When her father had divorced her first mother, Yoshiko had been four and her younger brother two. The reasons given for the divorce were that her mother went around dressed in flashy clothes and spent money wildly, but Yoshiko sensed dimly that it was more than that, that the real cause lay deeper down.

Her brother, as a child, had come across a photograph of their mother and shown it to their father. The father hadn't said anything but, with a face of terrible anger, had suddenly torn the photograph to bits.

When Yoshiko was thirteen, she had welcomed the new mother to the house. Later, Yoshiko had come to think that her father had endured his loneliness for ten years for her sake. The second mother was a good person. A peaceful home life continued.

When the younger brother, entering upper school, began living away from home in a dormitory, his attitude toward his stepmother changed noticeably.

"Elder sister, I've met our mother. She's married and lives in Azabu. She's really beautiful. She was happy to see me."

Hearing this suddenly, Yoshiko could not say a word. Her face paled, and she began to tremble.

From the next room, her stepmother came in and sat down.

"It's a good thing, a good thing. It's not bad to meet your own mother. It's only natural. I've known for some time that this day would come. I don't think anything particular of it."

But the strength seemed to have gone out of her step-mother's body. To Yoshiko, her emaciated stepmother seemed pathetically frail and small.

Her brother abruptly got up and left. Yoshiko felt like smacking him.

"Yoshiko, don't say anything to him. Speaking to him will only make that boy go bad." Her stepmother spoke in a low voice.

Tears came to Yoshiko's eyes.

Her father summoned her brother back home from the dormitory. Although Yoshiko had thought that would settle the matter, her father had then gone off to live elsewhere with her stepmother.

It had frightened Yoshiko. It was as if she had been crushed by the power of masculine indignation and resent-ment. Did their father dislike even them because of their tie to their first mother? It seemed to her that her brother, who'd got-ten to his feet so abruptly, had inherited the frightening male intransigence of his father.

And yet it also seemed to Yoshiko that she could now understand her father's sadness and pain during those ten years between his divorce and remarriage.

And so, when her father, who had moved away from her, came back bringing a marriage proposal, Yoshiko had been surprised.

"I've caused you a great deal of trouble. I told the young man's mother that you're a girl with these circumstances and that, rather than treating you like a bride, she should try to bring back the happy days of your childhood."

When her father said this kind of thing to her, Yoshiko wept.

If Yoshiko married, there would be no woman's hand to take care of her brother and grandmother. It had been decided that the two households would become one. With that, Yoshiko had made up her mind. She had dreaded marriage on her father's account, but, when it came down to the actual talks, it was not that dreadful after all.

When her preparations were completed, Yoshiko went to her grandmother's room.

"Grandmother, can you see the red in this kimono?"

"I can faintly make out some red over there. Which is it, now?" Pulling Yoshiko to her, the grandmother put her eyes close to the kimono and the sash.

"I've already forgotten your face, Yoshiko. I wish I could see what you look like now."

Yoshiko stifled a desire to giggle. She rested her hand lightly on her grandmother's head.

Wanting to go out and meet her father and the others, Yoshiko was unable just to sit there, vaguely waiting. She went out into the garden. She held out her hand, palm upward, but the rain was so fine that it didn't wet the palm. Gathering up the skirts of her kimono, Yoshiko assiduously searched among the little trees and in the bear-grass bamboo thicket. And there, in the tall grass under the bush clover, was the baby bird.

Her heart beating fast, Yoshiko crept nearer. The baby jay, drawing its head into its neck feathers, did not stir. It was easy to take it up into her hand. It seemed to have lost its energy. Yoshiko looked around her, but the mother bird was nowhere in sight.

Running into the house, Yoshiko called out, "Grandmother! I've found the baby bird. I have it in my hand. It's very weak."

"Oh, is that so? Try giving it some water."

Her grandmother was calm.

When she ladled some water into a rice bowl and dipped the baby jay's beak in it, it drank, its little throat swelling out in

an appealing way. Then—had it recovered?—it sang out, "Ki-ki-
ki, Ki-ki-ki . . ."

The mother bird, evidently hearing its cry, came flying.
Perching on the telephone wire, it sang. The baby bird, struggling in Yoshiko's hand, sang out again, "Ki-ki-ki . . ."

"Ah, how good that she came! Give it back to its mother,
quick," her grandmother said.

Yoshiko went back out into the garden. The mother bird
flew up from the telephone wire but kept her distance, looking
fixedly toward Yoshiko from the top of a cherry tree.

As if to show her the baby jay in her palm, Yoshiko raised
her hand, then quietly placed the chick on the ground.

As Yoshiko watched from behind the glass door, the mother
bird, guided by the voice of its child singing plaintively and looking up at the sky, gradually came closer. When she'd come down
to the low branch of a nearby pine, the chick flapped its wings,
trying to fly up to her. Stumbling forward in its efforts, falling all
over itself, it kept singing.

Still the mother bird cautiously held off from hopping
down to the ground.

Soon, however, it flew in a straight line to the side of its
child. The chick's joy was boundless. Turning and turning its
head, its outspread wings trembling, it made up to its mother.
Evidently the mother had brought it something to eat.

Yoshiko wished that her father and stepmother would
come soon. She would like to show them this, she thought.

—TRANSLATED BY LANE DUNLOP

AND J. MARTIN HOLMAN

THE BALEK SCALES

Heinrich Böll

GERMANY

Where my grandfather came from, most of the people lived by working in the flax sheds. For five generations they had been breathing in the dust which rose from the crushed flax stalks, letting themselves be killed off by slow degrees, a race of long-suffering, cheerful people who ate goat cheese, potatoes, and now and then a rabbit; in the evening they would sit at home spinning and knitting; they sang, drank mint tea, and were happy. During the day they would carry the flax stalks to the antiquated machines, with no protection from the dust and at the mercy of the heat which came pouring out of the drying kilns. Each cottage contained only one bed, standing against the wall like a closet and reserved for the parents, while the children slept all round the room on benches. In the morning the room would be filled with the odor of thin soup; on Sundays there was stew, and on feast days the children's faces would light up with pleasure as they watched the black acorn coffee turning paler and paler from the milk their smiling mother poured into their coffee mugs.

The parents went off early to the flax sheds, the housework was left to the children: they would sweep the room, tidy up, wash the dishes, and peel the potatoes, precious pale-yellow fruit whose thin peel had to be produced afterwards to dispel any suspicion of extravagance or carelessness.

As soon as the children were out of school they had to go off into the woods and, depending on the season, gather mushrooms and herbs: woodruff and thyme, caraway, mint, and foxglove, and in summer, when they had brought in the hay from their meager fields, they gathered hayflowers. A kilo of hayflowers was worth one pfennig, and they were sold by the apothecaries in town for twenty pfennigs a kilo to highly strung ladies. The mushrooms were highly prized: they fetched twenty pfennigs a kilo and were sold in the shops in town for one mark twenty. The children would crawl deep into the green darkness of the forest during the autumn when dampness drove the mushrooms out of the soil, and almost every family had its own places where it gathered mushrooms, places which were handed down in whispers from generation to generation.

The woods belonged to the Baleks, as well as the flax sheds, and in my grandfather's village the Baleks had a chateau, and the wife of the head of the family had a little room next to the dairy where mushrooms, herbs, and hayflowers were weighed and paid for. There on the table stood the great Balek scales, an old-fashioned, ornate bronze-gilt contraption, which my grandfather's grandparents had already faced when they were children, their grubby hands holding their little baskets of mushrooms, their paper bags of hayflowers, breathlessly watching the number of weights Frau Balek had to throw on the scale before the swinging pointer came to rest exactly over the black line, that thin line of justice which had to be redrawn every year. Then Frau Balek would take the big book covered in brown leather, write down the weight, and pay out the money, pfennigs or ten-pfennig pieces and very, very occasionally, a mark. And when my grandfather was a child there was a big glass jar of lemon drops standing there, the kind that cost one

mark a kilo, and when Frau Balek—whichever one happened to
be presiding over the little room—was in a good mood, she
would put her hand into this jar and give each child a lemon
drop, and the children's faces would light up with pleasure, the
way they used to when on feast days their mother poured milk
into their coffee mugs, milk that made the coffee turn paler and
paler until it was as pale as the flaxen pigtails of the little girls.
One of the laws imposed by the Baleks on the village was:
no one was permitted to have any scales in the house. The law
was so ancient that nobody gave a thought as to when and how it
had arisen, and it had to be obeyed, for anyone who broke it was
dismissed from the flax sheds, he could not sell his mushrooms
or his thyme or his hayflowers, and the power of the Baleks was
so far-reaching that no one in the neighboring villages would give
him work either, or buy his forest herbs. But since the days when
my grandfather's parents had gone out as small children to gather
mushrooms and sell them in order that they might season the
meat of the rich people of Prague or be baked into game pies, it
had never occurred to anyone to break this law: flour could be
measured in cups, eggs could be counted, what they had spun
could be measured by the yard, and besides, the old-fashioned,
bronze-gilt, ornate Balek scales did not look at if there was anything wrong with them, and five generations had entrusted the
swinging black pointer with what they had gone out as eager children to gather from the woods.
   True, there were some among these quiet people who
flouted the law, poachers bent on making more money in one
night than they could earn in a whole month in the flax sheds,
but even these people apparently never thought of buying
scales or making their own. My grandfather was the first person bold enough to test the justice of the Baleks, the family
who lived in the chateau and drove two carriages, who always
maintained one boy from the village while he studied theology

at the seminary in Prague, the family with whom the priest played taroc every Wednesday, on whom the local reeve, in his carriage emblazoned with the Imperial coat-of-arms, made an annual New Year's Day call and on whom the Emperor conferred a title on the first day of the year 1900.

My grandfather was hard-working and smart: he crawled further into the woods than the children of his clan had crawled before him, he penetrated as far as the thicket where, according to legend, Bilgan the Giant was supposed to dwell, guarding a treasure. But my grandfather was not afraid of Bilgan: he worked his way deep into the thicket, even when he was quite little, and brought out great quantities of mushrooms; he even found truffles, for which Frau Balek paid thirty pfennigs a pound. Everything my grandfather took to the Baleks he entered on the back of a torn-off calendar page: every pound of mushrooms, every gram of thyme, and on the right-hand side, in his childish handwriting, he entered the amount he received for each item; he scrawled in every pfennig, from the age of seven to the age of twelve, and by the time he was twelve the year 1900 had arrived, and because the Baleks had been raised to the aristocracy by the Emperor, they gave every family in the village a quarter of a pound of real coffee, the Brazilian kind; there was also free beer and tobacco for the men, and at the chateau there was a great banquet; many carriages stood in the avenue of poplars leading from the entrance gates to the chateau.

But the day before the banquet the coffee was distributed in the little room which had housed the Balek scales for almost a hundred years, and the Balek family was now called Balek von Bilgan because, according to legend, Bilgan the Giant used to have a great castle on the site of the present Balek estate.

My grandfather often used to tell me how he went there after school to fetch the coffee for four families: the Cechs, the Weidlers, the Vohlas, and his own, the Brüchers. It was the afternoon of New Year's Eve: there were the front rooms to be decorated, the baking to be done, and the families did not want to spare four boys and have each of them go all the way to the chateau to bring back a quarter of a pound of coffee. And so my grandfather sat on the narrow wooden bench in the little room while Gertrud the maid counted out the wrapped four-ounce packages of coffee, four of them, and he looked at the scales and saw that the pound weight was still lying on the left-hand scale; Frau Balek von Bilgan was busy with preparations for the banquet. And when Gertrud was about to put her hand into the jar with the lemon drops to give my grandfather one, she discovered it was empty: it was refilled once a year, and held one kilo of the kind that cost a mark.

Gertrud laughed and said: "Wait here while I get the new lot," and my grandfather waited with the four four-ounce packages which had been wrapped and sealed in the factory, facing the scales on which someone had left the pound weight, and my grandfather took the four packages of coffee, put them on the empty scale, and his heart thudded as he watched the black finger of justice come to rest on the left of the black line: the scale with the pound weight stayed down, and the pound of coffee remained up in the air; his heart thudded more than if he had been lying behind a bush in the forest waiting for Bilgan the Giant, and he felt in his pocket for the pebbles he always carried with him so he could use his catapult to shoot the sparrows which pecked away at his mother's cabbage plants—he had to put three, four, five pebbles beside the packages of coffee before the scale with the pound weight rose and the pointer at last came to rest over the black line. My grandfather took the coffee from the scale, wrapped the five pebbles in his kerchief, and when Gertrud came back with the big kilo bag of lemon drops which had to last for another whole year in order to make the children's faces light up with pleasure, when Gertrud let the lemon drops rattle into the glass jar, the pale little fellow was still standing there, and nothing seemed to have changed. My grandfather only took three of the packages, then Gertrud looked in startled surprise at the white-faced child who threw the lemon drop onto the floor, ground it under his heel, and said: "I want to see Frau Balek."

"Balek von Bilgan, if you please," said Gertrud.

"All right, Frau Balek von Bilgan," but Gertrud only laughed at him, and he walked back to the village in the dark, took the Cechs, the Weidlers, and the Vohlas their coffee, and said he had to go and see the priest.

Instead he went out into the dark night with his five pebbles in his kerchief. He had to walk a long way before he found someone who had scales, who was permitted to have them; no one in the villages of Blaugau and Bernau had any, he knew that, and he went straight through them till, after two hours' walking, he reached the little town of Dielheim where Honig the apothecary lived. From Honig's house came the smell of fresh pancakes, and Honig's breath, when he opened the door to the half-frozen boy, already smelled of punch, there was a moist cigar between his narrow lips, and he clasped the boy's cold hands firmly for a moment, saying: "What's the matter, has your father's lung got worse?"

"No, I haven't come for medicine, I wanted . . ." My grandfather undid his kerchief, took out the five pebbles, held them out to Honig, and said: "I wanted to have these weighed." He glanced anxiously into Honig's face, but when Honig said nothing and did not get angry, or even ask him anything, my grandfather said: "It is the amount that is short of justice," and now, as he went into the warm room, my grandfather realized how wet his feet were. The snow had soaked through his cheap shoes, and in the forest the branches had showered him with snow which was now melting, and he was tired and hungry and suddenly began to cry because he thought of the quantities of mushrooms, the herbs, the flowers, which had been weighed on the scales which were short five pebbles' worth of justice. And when Honig, shaking his head and holding the five pebbles, called his wife, my grandfather thought of the generations of his parents, his grandparents, who had all had to have their mushrooms, their flowers, weighed on the scales, and he was overwhelmed by a great wave of injustice, and began to sob louder than ever, and, without waiting to be asked, he sat down on a chair, ignoring the pancakes, the cup of hot coffee which nice plump Frau Honig put in front of him, and did not stop crying till Honig himself came out from the shop at the back and, rattling the pebbles in his hand, said in a low voice to his wife: "Fifty-five grams, exactly."

My grandfather walked the two hours home through the forest, got a beating at home, said nothing, not a single word, when he was asked about the coffee, spent the whole evening doing sums on the piece of paper on which he had written down everything he had sold to Frau Balek, and when midnight struck, and the cannon could be heard from the chateau, and the whole village rang with shouting and laughter and the noise of rattles, when the family kissed and embraced all round, he said into the New Year silence: "The Baleks owe me eighteen marks and thirty-two pfennigs." And again he thought of all the children there were in the village, of his brother Fritz who had gathered so many mushrooms, of his sister Ludmilla; he thought of the many hundreds of children who had all gathered mushrooms for the Baleks, and herbs and flowers, and this time he did not cry but told his parents and brothers and sisters of his discovery.

When the Baleks von Bilgan went to High Mass on New Year's Day, their new coat-of-arms—a giant crouching under a fir tree—already emblazoned in blue and gold on their carriage, they saw the hard, pale faces of the people all staring at them. They had expected garlands in the village, a song in their honor, cheers and hurrahs, but the village was completely deserted as they drove through it, and in church the pale faces of the people were turned toward them, mute and hostile, and when the priest mounted the pulpit to deliver his New Year's sermon he sensed the chill in those otherwise quiet and peaceful faces, and he stumbled painfully through his sermon and went back to the altar drenched in sweat. And as the Baleks von Bilgan left the church after Mass, they walked through a lane of mute, pale faces. But young Frau Balek von Bilgan stopped in front of the children's pews, sought out my grandfather's face, pale little Franz Brücher, and asked him, right there in the church: "Why didn't you take the coffee for your mother?" And my grand-father stood up and said: "Because you owe me as much money as five kilos of coffee would cost." And he pulled the five peb-bles from his pocket, held them out to the young woman, and said: "This much, fifty-five grams, is short in every pound of your justice"; and before the woman could say anything the men and women in the church lifted up their voices and sang: "The justice of this earth, O Lord, hath put Thee to death. . . ."

While the Baleks were at church, Wilhelm Vohla, the poacher, had broken into the little room, stolen the scales and the big fat leatherbound book in which had been entered every kilo of mushrooms, every kilo of hayflowers, everything bought by the Baleks in the village, and all afternoon of that New Year's Day the men of the village sat in my great-grandparents' front room and calculated, calculated one tenth of everything that had been bought—but when they had calculated many thou-sands of talers and had still not come to an end, the reeve's gen-darmes arrived, made their way into my great-grandfather's front room, shooting and stabbing as they came, and removed the scales and the book by force. My grandfather's little sister

Ludmilla lost her life, a few men were wounded, and one of the gendarmes was stabbed to death by Wilhelm Vohla the poacher.

Our village was not the only one to rebel: Blaugau and Bernau did too, and for almost a week no work was done in the flax sheds. But a great many gendarmes appeared, and the men and women were threatened with prison, and the Baleks forced the priest to display the scales publicly in the school and demonstrate that the finger of justice swung to and fro accurately. And the men and women went back to the flax sheds—but no one went to the school to watch the priest: he stood there all alone, helpless and forlorn with his weights, scales, and packages of coffee.

And the children went back to gathering mushrooms, to gathering thyme, flowers, and foxglove, but every Sunday, as soon as the Baleks entered the church, the hymn was struck up: "The justice of this earth, O Lord, hath put Thee to death," until the reeve ordered it proclaimed in every village that the singing of this hymn was forbidden.

My grandfather's parents had to leave the village, and the new grave of their little daughter; they became basket weavers, but did not stay long anywhere because it pained them to see how everywhere the finger of justice swung falsely. They walked along behind their cart, which crept slowly over the country roads, taking their thin goat with them, and passers-by could sometimes hear a voice from the cart singing: "The justice of this earth, O Lord, hath put Thee to death." And those who wanted to listen could hear the tale of the Baleks von Bilgan, whose justice lacked a tenth part. But there were few who listened.

—TRANSLATED BY LEILA VENNEWITZ

GAMES AT TWILIGHT

Anita Desai

INDIA

It was still too hot to play outdoors. They had had their tea, they had been washed and had their hair brushed, and after the long day of confinement in the house that was not cool but at least a protection from the sun, the children strained to get out. Their faces were red and bloated with the effort, but their mother would not open the door, everything was still curtained and shuttered in a way that stifled the children, made them feel that their lungs were stuffed with cotton wool and their noses with dust and if they didn't burst out into the light and see the sun and feel the air, they would choke.

"Please, Ma, please," they begged. "We'll play in the veranda and porch—we won't go a step out of the porch."

"You will, I know you will, and then—"

"No—we won't, we won't," they wailed so horrendously that she actually let down the bolt of the front door so that they burst out like seeds from a crackling, overripe pod into the veranda, with such wild, maniacal yells that she retreated to her bath and the shower of talcum powder and the fresh sari that were to help her face the summer evening.

They faced the afternoon. It was too hot. Too bright. The white walls of the veranda glared stridently in the sun. The bougainvillaea hung about it, purple and magenta, in livid balloons. The garden outside was like a tray made of beaten brass, flattened out on the red gravel and the stony soil in all shades of metal—aluminum, tin, copper, and brass. No life stirred at this arid time of day—the birds still drooped, like dead fruit, in the papery tents of the trees; some squirrels lay limp on the wet earth under the garden tap. The outdoor dog lay stretched as if dead on the veranda mat, his paws and ears and tail all reaching out like dying travelers in search of water. He rolled his eyes at the children—two white marbles rolling in the purple sockets, begging for sympathy—and attempted to lift his tail in a wag but could not. It only twitched and lay still.

Then, perhaps roused by the shrieks of the children, a band of parrots suddenly fell out of the eucalyptus tree, tumbled frantically in the still, sizzling air, then sorted themselves out into battle formation and streaked away across the white sky.

The children, too, felt released. They too began tumbling, shoving, pushing against each other, frantic to start. Start what? Start their business. The business of the children's day which is—play.

"Let's play hide-and-seek."

"Who'll be It?"

"You be It."

"Why should I? You be—"

"You're the eldest—"

"That doesn't mean—"

The shoves became harder. Some kicked out. The motherly Mira intervened. She pulled the boys roughly apart. There was a tearing sound of cloth but it was lost in the heavy panting and angry grumbling and no one paid attention to the small sleeve hanging loosely off a shoulder.

"Make a circle, make a circle!" she shouted, firmly pulling
and pushing till a kind of vague circle was formed. "Now clap!"
she roared and, clapping, they all chanted in melancholy uni-
son: "Dip, dip, dip—my blue ship—" and every now and then
one or the other saw he was safe by the way his hands fell at
the crucial moment—palm on palm, or back of hand on palm—
and dropped out of the circle with a yell and a jump of relief
and jubilation.

Raghu was It. He started to protest, to cry, "You cheated—
Mira cheated—Anu cheated—" but it was too late, the others
had already streaked away. There was no one to hear when he
called out, "Only in the veranda—the porch—Ma said—Ma
said to stay in the porch!" No one had stopped to listen, all he
saw were their brown legs flashing through the dusty shrubs,
scrambling up brick walls, leaping over compost heaps and
hedges, and then the porch stood empty in the purple shade of
the bougainvillaea and the garden was as empty as before; even
the limp squirrels had whisked away, leaving everything gleam-
ing, brassy and bare.

Only small Manu suddenly reappeared, as if he had
dropped out of an invisible cloud or from a bird's claws, and
stood for a moment in the center of the yellow lawn, chewing
his finger and near to tears as he heard Raghu shouting, with
his head pressed against the veranda wall, "Eighty-three,
eighty-five, eighty-nine, ninety . . ." and then made off in a
panic, half of him wanting to fly north, the other half counsel-
ing south. Raghu turned just in time to see the flash of his
white shorts and the uncertain skittering of his red sandals,
and charged after him with such a bloodcurdling yell that Manu
stumbled over the hosepipe, fell into its rubber coils, and lay
there weeping, "I won't be It—you have to find them all—all—
all!"

"I know I have to, idiot," Raghu said, superciliously kicking him with his toe. "You're dead," he said with satisfaction, licking the beads of perspiration off his upper lip, and then stalked off in search of worthier prey, whistling spiritedly so that the hiders should hear and tremble.

Ravi heard the whistling and picked his nose in a panic, trying to find comfort by burrowing the finger deep-deep into that soft tunnel. He felt himself too exposed, sitting on an upturned flowerpot behind the garage. Where could he burrow? He could run around the garage if he heard Raghu come—around and around and around—but he hadn't much faith in his short legs when matched against Raghu's long, hefty, hairy footballer legs. Ravi had a frightening glimpse of them as Raghu combed the hedge of crotons and hibiscus, trampling delicate ferns underfoot as he did so. Ravi looked about him desperately, swallowing a small ball of snot in his fear.

The garage was locked with a great heavy lock to which the driver had the key in his room, hanging from a nail on the wall under his work-shirt. Ravi had peeped in and seen him still sprawling on his string-cot in his vest and striped underpants, the hair on his chest and the hair in his nose shaking with the vibrations of his phlegm-obstructed snores. Ravi had wished he were tall enough, big enough, to reach the key on the nail, but it was impossible, beyond his reach for years to come. He had sidled away and sat dejectedly on the flowerpot. That at least was cut to his own size.

But next to the garage was another shed with a big green door. Also locked. No one even knew who had the key to the lock. That shed wasn't opened more than once a year when Ma turned out all the old broken bits of furniture and rolls of matting and leaking buckets, and the white ant hills were broken and swept away and Flit sprayed into the spider webs and rat holes so that the whole operation was like the looting of a poor, ruined, and conquered city. The green leaves of the door sagged. They were nearly off their rusty hinges. The hinges were large and made a small gap between the door and the walls—only just large enough for rats, dogs, and, possibly, Ravi to slip through.

Ravi had never cared to enter such a dark and depressing mortuary of defunct household goods seething with such unspeakable and alarming animal life but, as Raghu's whistling grew angrier and sharper and his crashing and storming in the hedge wilder, Ravi suddenly slipped off the flowerpot and through the crack and was gone. He chuckled aloud with astonishment at his own temerity so that Raghu came out of the hedge, stood silent with his hands on his hips, listening, and finally shouted, "I heard you! I'm coming! *Got* you—" and came charging round the garage only to find the upturned flowerpot, the yellow dust, the crawling of white ants in a mid-hill against the closed shed door—nothing. Snarling, he bent to pick up a stick and went off, whacking it against the garage and shed walls as if to beat out his prey.

Ravi shook, then shivered with delight, with self-congratulation. Also with fear. It was dark, spooky in the shed. It had a muffled smell, as of graves. Ravi had once got locked into the linen cupboard and sat there weeping for half an hour before he was rescued. But at least that had been a familiar place, and even smelt pleasantly of starch, laundry, and, reassuringly, of his mother. But the shed smelt of rats, ant hills, dust, and spider webs. Also of less definable, less recognizable, horrors. And it was dark. Except for the white-hot cracks along the door, there was no light. The roof was very low. Although Ravi was small, he felt as if he could reach up and touch it with his fingertips. But he didn't stretch. He hunched himself into a ball so as not to bump into anything, touch or feel anything. What might there not be to touch him and feel him as he stood there, trying to see in the dark? Something cold, or slimy—like a snake. Snakes! He leapt up as Raghu whacked the wall with his stick—then, quickly realizing what it was, felt almost relieved to hear Raghu, hear his stick. It made him feel protected.

But Raghu soon moved away. There wasn't a sound once his footsteps had gone around the garage and disappeared. Ravi stood frozen inside the shed. Then he shivered all over. Something had tickled the back of his neck. It took him a while to pick up the courage to lift his hand and explore. It was an insect—perhaps a spider—exploring *him*. He squashed it and wondered how many more creatures were watching him, waiting to reach out and touch him, the stranger.

There was nothing now. After standing in that position— his hand still on his neck, feeling the wet splodge of the squashed spider gradually dry—for minutes, hours, his legs began to tremble with the effort, the inaction, By now he could see enough in the dark to make out the large solid shapes of old wardrobes, broken buckets, and bedsteads piled on top of each other around him. He recognized an old bathtub—patches of enamel glimmered at him and at last he lowered himself on to its edge.

He contemplated slipping out of the shed and into the fray. He wondered if it would not be better to be captured by Raghu and be returned to the milling crowd as long as he could be in the sun, the light, the free spaces of the garden and the familiarity of his brothers, sisters, and cousins. It would be evening soon. Their games would become legitimate. The parents would sit out on the lawn on cane basket chairs and watch them as they tore around the garden or gathered in knots to share a loot of mulberries or black, teeth-splitting *jamun* from the garden trees. The gardener would fix the hosepipe to the water tap and water would fall lavishly through the air to the ground, soaking the dry yellow grass and the red gravel and arousing the sweet, the intoxicating, scent of water on dry earth—that loveliest scent in the world. Ravi sniffed for a whiff of it. He half-rose from the bathtub, then heard the despairing scream of one of the girls as Raghu bore down upon her. There was the sound of a crash, and of rolling about in the bushes, the shrubs, then screams and accusing sobs of "I touched the den—" "You did not—" "I did—" "You liar, you did *not*," and then a fading away and silence again.

Ravi sat back on the harsh edge of the tub, deciding to hold out a bit longer. What fun if they were all found and caught—he alone left unconquered! He had never known that sensation. Nothing more wonderful had ever happened to him than being taken out by an uncle and bought a whole slab of chocolate all to himself, or being flung into the soda-man's pony cart and driven up to the gate by the friendly driver with the red beard and pointed ears. To defeat Raghu—that hirsute, hoarse-voiced football champion—and to be the winner in a circle of older, bigger, luckier children—that would be thrilling beyond imagination. He hugged his knees together and smiled to himself almost shyly at the thought of so much victory, such laurels.

There he sat smiling, knocking his heels against the bathtub, now and then getting up and going to the door to put his ear to the broad crack and listening for sounds of the game, the pursuer and the pursued, and then returning to his seat with the dogged determination of the true winner, a breaker of records, a champion.

It grew darker in the shed as the light at the door grew softer, fuzzier, turned to a kind of crumbling yellow pollen that turned to yellow fur, blue fur, gray fur. Evening. Twilight. The sound of water gushing, falling. The scent of earth receiving

water, slaking its thirst in great gulps and releasing that green
scent of freshness, coolness. Through the crack Ravi saw the
long purple shadows of the shed and the garage lying still
across the yard. Beyond that, the white walls of the house. The
bougainvillaea had lost its lividity, hung in dark bundles that
quaked and twittered and seethed with masses of homing sparrows. The lawn was shut off from his view. Could he hear the
children's voices? It seemed to him that he could. It seemed to
him that he could hear them chanting, singing, laughing. But
what about the game? What had happened? Could it be over?
How could it when he was still not found?

It then occurred to him that he could have slipped out
long ago, dashed across the yard to the veranda and touched
the den. It was necessary to do that to win. He had forgotten.
He had only remembered the part of hiding and trying to elude
the seeker. He had done that so successfully, his success had
occupied him so wholly, that he had quite forgotten that success had to be clinched by that final dash to victory and the
ringing cry of "Den!"

With a whimper he burst through the crack, fell on his
knees, got up and stumbled on stiff, benumbed legs across the
shadowy yard, crying heartily by the time he reached the veranda so that when he flung himself at the white pillar and bawled,
"Den! Den! Den!" his voice broke with rage and pity at the disgrace of it all and he felt himself flooded with tears and misery.

Out on the lawn, the children stopped chanting. They all
turned to stare at him in amazement. Their faces were pale and
triangular in the dusk. The trees and bushes around them stood
inky and sepulchral, spilling long shadows across them. They
stared, wondering at his reappearance, his passion, his wild
animal howling. Their mother rose from her basket chair and
came towards him, worried, annoyed, saying, "Stop it, stop it,
Ravi. Don't be a baby. Have you hurt yourself?" Seeing him

attended to, the children went back to clasping their hands and chanting "The grass is green, the rose is red . . ."

But Ravi would not let them. He tore himself out of his mother's grasp and pounded across the lawn into their midst, charging at them with his head lowered so that they scattered in surprise. "I won, I won, I won," he bawled, shaking his head so that the big tears flew. "Raghu didn't find me. I won, I won—"

It took them a minute to grasp what he was saying, even who he was. They had quite forgotten him. Raghu had found all the others long ago. There had been a fight about who was to be It next. It had been so fierce that their mother had emerged from her bath and made them change to another game. Then they had played another and another. Broken mulberries from the tree and eaten them. Helped the driver wash the car when their father returned from work. Helped the gardener water the beds till he roared at them and swore he would complain to their parents. The parents had come out, taken up their positions on the cane chairs. They had begun to play again, sing and chant. All this time no one had remembered Ravi. Having disappeared from the scene, he had disappeared from their minds. Clean.

"Don't be a fool," Raghu said roughly, pushing him aside, and even Mira said, "Stop howling, Ravi. If you want to play, you can stand at the end of the line," and she put him there very firmly.

The game proceeded. Two pairs of arms reached up and met in an arc. The children trooped under it again and again in a lugubrious circle, ducking their heads and intoning,

> *The grass is green, the rose is red;*
> *Remember me when I am dead, dead, dead, dead . . .*

And the arc of thin arms trembled in the twilight, and the heads were bowed so sadly, and their feet tramped to that melancholy refrain so mournfully, so helplessly, that Ravi could not bear it. He would not follow them, he would not be included in this funereal game. He had wanted victory and triumph—not a funeral. But he had been forgotten, left out, and he would not join them now. The ignominy of being forgotten—how could he face it? He felt his heart go heavy and ache inside him unbearably. He lay down full length on the damp grass, crushing his face into it, no longer crying, silenced by a terrible sense of his insignificance.

THE LATE BUD

Ama Ata Aidoo

GHANA

"The good child who willingly goes on errands eats the food of peace." This was a favorite saying in the house. Maami, Aunt Efua, Aunt Araba . . . oh, they all said it, especially when they had prepared something delicious like cocoyam porridge and seasoned beef. You know how it is.

First, as they stirred it with the ladle, its scent rose from the pot and became a little cloud hanging over the hearth. Gradually, it spread through the courtyard and entered the inner and outer rooms of the women's apartments. This was the first scent that greeted the afternoon sleeper. She stretched herself luxuriously, inhaled a large quantity of the sweet scent, cried "Mm," and either fell back again to sleep or got up to be about her business. The aroma did not stay. It rolled into the next house and the next, until it filled the whole neighborhood. And Yaaba would sniff it.

As usual, she would be playing with her friends by the Big Trunk. She would suddenly throw down her pebbles even if it was her turn, jump up, shake her cloth free of sand, and announce, "I am going home."

"Why?"

"Yaaba, why?"

But the questions of her amazed companions would reach her faintly like whispers. She was flying home. Having crossed the threshold, she then slunk by the wall. But there would be none for her.

Yaaba never stayed at home to go on an errand. Even when she was around, she never would fetch water to save a dying soul. How could she then eat the food of peace? Oh, if it was a formal meal, like in the morning or evening, that was a different matter. Of that, even Yaaba got her lawful share. . . . But not this sweet-sweet porridge. "Nsia, Antobam, Naabanyin, Adwoa, come for some porridge." And the other children trooped in with their little plates and bowls. But not the figure by the wall. They chattered as they came and the mother teased as she dished out their tidbits.

"Is yours all right, Adwoa? . . . and yours, Tawia? . . . yours is certainly sufficient, Antobam. . . . But my child, this is only a tidbit for us, the deserving. Other people," and she would squint at Yaaba, "who have not worked will not get the tiniest bit." She then started eating hers. If Yaaba felt that the joke was being carried too far, she coughed. "Oh," the mother would cry out, "people should be careful about their throats. Even if they coughed until they spat blood none of this porridge would touch their mouths."

But it was not things and incidents like these which worried Yaaba. For inevitably, a mother's womb cried out for a lonely figure by a wall and she would be given some porridge. Even when her mother could be bile-bellied enough to look at her and dish out all the porridge, Yaaba could run into the doorway and ambush some child and rob him of the greater part of his share. No, it was not such things that worried her. Every mother might call her a bad girl. She enjoyed playing by the Big Trunk, for instance. Since to be a good girl, one had to stay by the hearth and not by the Big Trunk throwing pebbles, but with one's hands folded quietly on one's lap, waiting to be sent everywhere by all the mothers, Yaaba let people like Adwoa who wanted to be called "good" be good. Thank you, she was not interested.

But there was something which disturbed Yaaba. No one knew it did, but it did. She used to wonder why, every time Maami called Adwoa, she called her "My child Adwoa," while she was always merely called "Yaaba."

"My child Adwoa, pick me the drinking can. . . . My child, you have done well. . . ."

Oh, it is so always. Am I not my mother's child?

"Yaaba, come for your food." She always wished in her heart that she could ask somebody about it. . . . Paapa . . . Maami . . . Nana, am I not Maami's daughter? Who was my mother?

But you see, one does not go around asking elders such questions. Take the day Antobam asked her grandmother where her own mother was. The grandmother also asked Antobam whether she was not being looked after well, and then started weeping and saying things. Other mothers joined in the weeping. Then some more women came over from the neighborhood and her aunts and uncles came too and there was more weeping and there was also drinking and libation-pouring. At the end of it all, they gave Antobam a stiff talking-to.

No, one does not go round asking one's elders such questions.

But Adwoa, my child, bring me the knife. . . . Yaaba . . . Yaaba, your cloth is dirty. Yaaba, Yaaba . . .

It was the afternoon of the Saturday before Christmas Sunday. Yaaba had just come from the playgrounds to gobble down her afternoon meal. It was kenkey and a little fish stewed in palm oil. She had eaten in such a hurry that a bone had got stuck in her throat. She had drunk a lot of water but still the bone was sticking there. She did not want to tell Maami about it. She knew she would get a scolding or even a knock on the head. It was while she was in the outer room looking for a bit of kenkey to push down the troublesome bone that she heard Maami talking in the inner room.

"Ah, and what shall I do now? But I thought there was a whole big lump left. . . . O . . . O! Things like this irritate me so. How can I spend Christmas without varnishing my floor?"

Yaaba discovered a piece of kenkey which was left from the week before, hidden in its huge wrappings. She pounced upon it and without breaking away the mildew, swallowed it. She choked, stretched her neck, and the bone was gone. She drank some water and with her cloth, wiped away the tears which had started gathering in her eyes. She was about to bounce away to the playgrounds when she remembered that she had heard Maami speaking to herself.

Although one must not stand by to listen to elders if they are not addressing one, yet one can hide and listen. And anyway, it would be interesting to hear the sort of things our elders say to themselves. "And how can I celebrate Christmas on a hardened, whitened floor?" Maami's voice went on. "If I could only get a piece of red earth. But I cannot go round my friends begging, 'Give me a piece of red earth.' No. O . . . O! And it is growing dark already. If only my child Adwoa was here. I am sure she could have run to the red-earth pit and fetched me just a hoeful. Then I could varnish the floor before the church bells ring tomorrow." Yaaba was thinking she had heard enough.

After all, our elders do not say anything interesting to themselves. It is their usual complaints about how difficult life is. If it is not the price of cloth or fish, then it is the scarcity of water. It is all very uninteresting. I will always play with my children when they grow up. I will not grumble about anything. . . .

It was quite dark. The children could hardly see their own

hands as they threw up the pebbles. But Yaaba insisted that
they go on. There were only three left of the eight girls who
were playing *soso-mba*. From time to time mothers, fathers, or
elder sisters had come and called to the others to go home. The
two still with Yaaba were Panyin and Kakra. Their mother had
traveled and that was why they were still there. No one came
any longer to call Yaaba. Up till the year before, Maami always
came to yell for her when it was sundown. When she could not
come, she sent Adwoa. But of course, Yaaba never listened to
them.

What is the point in breaking a game to go home? She
stayed out and played even by herself until it was dark and she
was satisfied. And now, at the age of ten, no one came to call
her.

The pebble hit Kakra on the head.

"*Ajii.*"

"What is it?"

"The pebble has hit me."

"I am sorry. It was not intentional." Panyin said, "But it is
dark, Kakra, let us go home." So they stood up.

"Panyin, will you go to church tomorrow?"

"No."

"Why? You have no new cloths?"

"We have new cloths but we will not get gold chains or
earrings. Our mother is not at home. She has gone to some
place and will only return in the afternoon. Kakra, remember
we will get up very early tomorrow morning."

"Why?"

"Have you forgotten what mother told us before she went
away? Did she not tell us to go and get some red earth from the
pit? Yaaba, we are going away."

"*Yoo.*"

And the twins turned towards home.

Red earth! The pit! Probably, Maami will be the only woman in the village who will not have red earth to varnish her floor. *Oo!*

"Panyin! Kakra! Panyin!"

"Who is calling us?"

"It is me, Yaaba. Wait for me."

She ran in the darkness and almost collided with someone who was carrying food to her husband's house.

"Panyin, do you say you will go to the pit tomorrow morning?"

"Yes, what is it?"

"I want to go with you."

"Why?"

"Because I want to get some red earth for my mother."

"But tomorrow you will go to church."

"Yes, but I will try to get it done in time to go to church as well."

"See, you cannot. Do you not know the pit? It is very far away. Everyone will already be at church by the time we get back home."

Yaaba stood quietly digging her right toe into the hard ground beneath her. "It doesn't matter, I will go."

"Do you not want to wear your gold things? Kakra and I are very sorry that we cannot wear ours because our mother is not here."

"It does not matter. Come and wake me up."

"Where do you sleep?"

"Under my mother's window. I will wake up if you hit the window with a small pebble."

"*Yoo.* . . . We will come to call you."

"Do not forget your *apampa* and your hoe."

"*Yoo.*"

When Yaaba arrived home, they had already finished eat-

ing the evening meal. Adwoa had arrived from an errand it
seemed. In fact she had gone on several others. Yaaba was
slinking like a cat to take her food which she knew would be
under the wooden bowl, when Maami saw her. "Yes, go and
take it. You are hungry, are you not? And very soon you will be
swallowing all that huge lump of fufu as quickly as a hen would
swallow corn." Yaaba stood still.

"*Aa*. My Father God, who inflicted on me such a child?
Look here, Yaaba. You are growing, so be careful how you live
your life. When you are ten years old you are not a child any
more. And a woman that lives on the playground is not a
woman. If you were a boy, it would be bad enough, but for a
girl, it is a curse. The house cannot hold you. *Tchia.*"

Yaaba crept into the outer room. She saw the wooden
bowl. She turned it over and as she had known all the time, her
food was there. She swallowed it more quickly than a hen
would have swallowed corn. When she finished eating, she
went into the inner room, she picked her mat, spread it on the
floor, threw herself down, and was soon asleep. Long afterwards, Maami came in from the conversation with the other
mothers. When she saw the figure of Yaaba, her heart did a
somersault. Pooh, went her fists on the figure in the corner.
Pooh, "You lazy lazy thing." Pooh, pooh! "You good-for-nothing,
empty cornhusk of a daughter . . ." She pulled her ears, and
Yaaba screamed. Still sleepy-eyed, she sat up on the mat.

"If you like, you scream, and watch what I will do to you.
If I do not pull your mouth until it is as long as a pestle, then
my name is not Benyiwa."

But Yaaba was now wide awake and tearless. Who said
she was screaming, anyway? She stared at Maami with shining
tearless eyes. Maami was angry at this too.

"I spit in your eyes, witch! Stare at me and tell me if I am
going to die tomorrow. At your age . . ." and the blows came

pooh, pooh, pooh. "You do not know that you wash yourself before your skin touches the mat. And after a long day in the sand, the dust and filth by the Big Trunk. *Hoo! Pooh!* You moth-bitten grain. *Pooh!*"

The clock in the chief's house struck twelve o'clock midnight. Yaaba never cried. She only tried, without success, to ward off the blows. Perhaps Maami was tired herself, perhaps she was satisfied. Or perhaps she was afraid she was putting herself in the position of Kweku Ananse tempting the spirits to carry their kindness as far as to come and help her beat her daughter. Of course, this would kill Yaaba. Anyway, she stopped beating her and lay down by Kofi, Kwame, and Adwoa. Yaaba saw the figure of Adwoa lying peacefully there. It was then her eyes misted. The tears flowed from her eyes. Every time, she wiped them with her cloth but more came. They did not make any noise for Maami to hear. Soon the cloth was wet. When the clock struck one, she heard Maami snoring. She herself could not sleep even when she lay down.

Is this woman my mother?

Perhaps I should not go and fetch her some red earth. But the twins will come. . . .

Yaaba rose and went into the outer room. There was no door between the inner and outer rooms to creak and wake anybody. She wanted the *apampa* and a hoe. At ten years of age, she should have had her own of both, but of course, she had not. Adwoa's hoe, she knew, was in the corner left of the door. She groped and found it. She also knew Adwoa's *apampa* was on the bamboo shelf. It was when she turned and was groping towards the bamboo shelf that she stumbled over the large water-bowl. Her chest hit the edge of the tray. The tray tilted and the water poured on the floor. She could not rise up. When Maami heard the noise her fall made, she screamed "Thief! Thief! Thief! Everybody, come, there is a thief in my room."

She gave the thief a chance to run away since he might attack her before the men of the village came. But no thief rushed through the door and there were no running footsteps in the courtyard. In fact, all was too quiet.

She picked up the lantern, pushed the wick up to blazing point, and went gingerly to the outer room. There was Yaaba, sprawled like a freshly killed overgrown cock on the tray. She screamed again.

"Ah Yaaba, why do you frighten me like this? What were you looking for? That is why I always say you are a witch. What do you want at this time of the night that you should fall on a water-bowl? And look at the floor. But of course, you were playing when someone lent me a piece of red earth to polish it, eh?" The figure in the tray just lay there. Maami bent down to help her up and then she saw the hoe. She stood up again.

"A hoe! I swear by all that be that I do not understand this." She lifted her up and was carrying her to the inner room when Yaaba's lips parted as if to say something. She closed the lips again, her eyelids fluttered down and the neck sagged. "My Savior!" There was nothing strange in the fact that the cry was heard in the north and south of the village. Was it not past midnight?

People had heard Maami's first cry of "Thief" and by the time she cried out again, the first men were coming from all directions. Soon the courtyard was full. Questions and answers went round. Some said Yaaba was trying to catch a thief, others that she was running from her mother's beating. But the first thing was to wake her up.

"Pour anowata into her nose!"—and the mothers ran into their husbands' chambers to bring their giant-sized bottles of the sweetest scents. "Touch her feet with a little fire.". . . "Squeeze a little ginger juice into her nose."

The latter was done and before she could suffer further ordeals, Yaaba's eyelids fluttered up.

"*Aa. . . . Oo . . .* we thank God. She is awake, she is awake." Everyone said it. Some were too far away and saw her neither in the faint nor awake. But they said it as they trooped back to piece together their broken sleep. Egya Yaw, the village medicine-man, examined her and told the now-mad Maami that she should not worry. "The impact was violent but I do not think anything has happened to the breastbone. I will bind her up in beaten herbs and she should be all right in a few days." "Thank you, Egya," said Maami, Paapa, her grandmother, the other mothers, and all her relatives. The medicine-man went to his house and came back. Yaaba's brawniest uncles beat up the herbs. Soon, Yaaba was bound up. The cock had crowed once, when they laid her down. Her relatives then left for their own homes. Only Maami, Paapa, and the other mothers were left. "And how is she?" one of the women asked.

"But what really happened?"

"Only Benyiwa can answer you."

"Benyiwa, what happened?"

"But I am surprised myself. After she had eaten her kenkey this afternoon, I heard her movements in the outer room but I did not mind her. Then she went away and came back when it was dark to eat her food. After our talk, I went to sleep. And there she was lying. As usual, she had not had a wash, so I just held her . . ."

"You held her what? Had she met with death you would have been the one that pushed her into it—beating a child in the night!"

"But Yaaba is too troublesome!"

"And so you think every child will be good? But how did she come to fall in the tray?"

"That is what I cannot tell. My eyes were just playing me tricks when I heard some noise in the outer room."

"Is that why you cried 'Thief'?"

"Yes. When I went to see what it was, I saw her lying in the tray, clutching a hoe."

"A hoe?"

"Yes, Adwoa's hoe."

"Perhaps there was a thief after all? She can tell us the truth . . . but . . ."

So they went on through the early morning. Yaaba slept. The second cock-crow came. The church bell soon did its Christmas reveille. In the distance, they heard the songs of the dawn procession. Quite near in the doorway, the regular pat, pat of the twins' footsteps drew nearer towards the elderly group by the hearth. Both parties were surprised at the encounter.

"Children, what do you want at dawn?"

"Where is Yaaba?"

"Yaaba is asleep."

"May we go and wake her, she asked us to."

"Why?"

"She said she will go with us to the red-earth pit."

"O . . . O!" The group around the hearth was amazed but they did not show it before the children.

"*Yoo.* You go today. She may come with you next time."

"*Yoo,* Mother."

"Walk well, my children. When she wakes up, we shall tell her you came."

"We cannot understand it. Yaaba? What affected her head?"

"My sister, the world is a strange place. That is all."

"And my sister, the child that will not do anything is better than a sheep."

"Benyiwa, we will go and lie down a little."

"Good morning."

"Good morning."

"Good morning."

"*Yoo.* I thank you all."

So Maami went into the apartment and closed the door. She knelt by the sleeping Yaaba and put her left hand on her bound chest. "My child, I say thank you. You were getting ready to go and fetch me red earth? Is that why you were holding the hoe? My child, my child, I thank you."

And the tears streamed down her face. Yaaba heard "My child" from very far away. She opened her eyes. Maami was weeping and still calling her "My child" and saying things which she did not understand.

Is Maami really calling me that? May the twins come. Am I Maami's own child?

"My child Yaaba . . ."

But how will I get red earth?

But why can I not speak . . .?

"I wish the twins would come . . ."

I want to wear the gold earrings . . .

I want to know whether Maami called me her child. Does it mean I am her child like Adwoa is? But one does not ask our elders such questions. And anyway, there is too much pain. And there are barriers where my chest is.

Probably tomorrow . . . but now Maami called me "My child!". . .

And she fell asleep again.

Valentin Rasputin

RUSSIA

In 1948 I entered fifth grade. To be more exact, I went away to
school. Since our village only had a four-year elementary
school, I had to pack up and leave home to continue my education in the nearest town, which was over fifty kilometers away.
My mother went there the week before and arranged for me to
room with a woman friend of hers. And on the last day of
August, Uncle Vanya, whose job was to drive our kolkhoz's
only pickup truck, dropped me off on Podkamennaya Street,
where I would be staying. He helped me carry my bedroll into
the house, gave me an encouraging farewell pat on the shoulder, and took off. And so, at the age of eleven, I began life on
my own.

Famine still held us in its grip that year, and my mother
had three kids to feed, with me being the oldest. In the spring,
when we were especially hungry, I had swallowed some potato
sprouts and grains of oats and rye, and I had made my sister
swallow them, too, in hopes of getting them to take root in our
stomachs—then we wouldn't have to think about food all the
time. We faithfully poured pure water from the Angara River on
those seeds all summer, but for some reason there was nothing
to harvest, or there was so little that we couldn't detect it.

Nevertheless, I don't think this was a totally useless venture, and some day it may even come in handy for the human race. Through inexperience we simply hadn't done it right.

It's hard to say just how Mother got up the courage to ship me off to town ("town" is what we called the county seat). Our father wasn't with us, we were quite poor, and she evidently figured that things couldn't possibly get any worse. I enjoyed going to school, did well in my studies, and was regarded in the village as a scholar. The old women had me write letters for them and read them the replies. I'd gone through all the books we had in our meager village library, and I would spend evenings reciting all manner of stories from them to the other kids—not only retelling them but also adding things on my own. But I was especially trusted when it came to the lottery. During the war, people had bought a lot of bonds, which doubled as lottery tickets. Columns of winning numbers were often printed, and then people would bring their bonds to me. They thought I had an eagle eye. Our village did have some winnings, mostly small ones, but in those years the collective farmers were thankful for each and every kopeck, and occasionally, with my assistance, they were blessed with completely unexpected good fortune. Their joy would automatically spill over onto me, too. They singled me out from the other village kids and even fed me. One time, after winning four hundred rubles, a fairly tightfisted, stingy old man named Uncle Ilya excitedly scraped together a bucket of potatoes for me, which in the springtime was quite a treasure.

And just because I had a knack for lottery numbers they used to say to my mother, "Your boy's got a good head on his shoulders. You oughta make sure he learns a thing or two. Schooling won't be lost on him."

So Mother, in spite of all our hardships, got me ready to leave, even though not a single kid from our village had ever gone to school in town before. I was the first. And I didn't fully realize what lay in store for me, what trials awaited me, poor fellow, in my new place of residence.

My schoolwork went well there, too. What else could I do? That's why I'd gone. I had no other business there, and I still hadn't learned to make light of the responsibilities that had been placed on me. I would not have dared to show up at school if even a single homework assignment hadn't been done, and so I got A's in all subjects, except French.

My problem with French was pronunciation. I had no trouble memorizing words and common expressions, I was quick at translation, and I coped splendidly with the intricacies of spelling, but pronunciation completely gave away my Angara origins, where down to the present generation no one has ever spoken foreign words, if they even suspect that such things exist. I spewed out French like a series of village tongue twisters, swallowing half the sounds, the nonessential ones, and blurting out the other half in short, barking bursts. Lidia Mikhaylovna, the French teacher, would frown helplessly when listening to me and close her eyes. She'd never heard anything like that, of course. Time and time again she would demonstrate how to pronounce the nasals and the vowel clusters. She'd ask me to repeat them—and I would panic. My tongue would stiffen in my mouth and refuse to budge. It was all to no avail. But the worst part began only when school was over. At school I was unwillingly distracted, under constant pressure to do things, and pestered by the other kids—I had to run around and play with them whether I wanted to or not. And in class I had to work. But whenever I was alone, homesickness immediately overwhelmed me—I missed the village, I missed my home. Before that I had never spent a single day away from my family and naturally I wasn't ready to live among total strangers. I felt so bad, so bitter and frustrated—it was worse than any illness. I had only one wish, one dream—to go home, just to go home. I lost a lot of weight, and when Mother came for a visit at the end of September, she became alarmed. While she was there I braced myself and didn't complain or cry, but when she was about to leave, I lost control and ran bawling after the truck. From inside the cab, Mother motioned me to go back and not disgrace both myself and her—this I couldn't comprehend at all. Then she changed her mind and had the driver stop.

"Get your stuff," she demanded when I ran up to the truck. "That's enough education for you. We're going home."

I came to my senses and ran back.

But it wasn't just homesickness that made me lose weight. Besides that, I still never got enough to eat. In the autumn, when Uncle Vanya was hauling grain in the pickup to the storage elevators not far from town, they would send me food quite often, about once a week. But the trouble was that I needed more. They had nothing to send except bread and potatoes. On rare occasions Mother would fill a jar with cottage cheese that she'd gotten by trading something, since she didn't have a cow of her own. Whenever they brought me food it seemed like a lot, but two days later I'd look, and it would all be gone. Very quickly I began to notice that at least half my bread was disappearing in a most mysterious manner. I checked—and sure enough, now you see it, now you don't. The same thing was happening to my potatoes. Who was stealing my food? Was it Aunt Nadya, that scolding, worn-out woman muddling along by herself with three kids? Was it one of her older girls, or maybe the boy, Fedka, her youngest? I didn't know who it was. I was afraid even to think about it, much less keep watch. It simply pained me because Mother was taking food from the family, from my little sister and brother, for my sake, and that food was somehow getting lost in the shuffle. But I forced myself to accept that, too, with humble resignation. Mother's life would not have been any easier if she had learned the truth.

Famine in town was not at all like famine in the country-side. There you could always find something to nibble at any time of year, especially in the autumn, when there'd be things to gather, dig up, and pick up from the ground. There were fish in the Angara and game birds in the forest. In town I felt sur-rounded by a complete void: strangers, strangers' gardens, strangers' land. Ten rows of small fishnets lay across a little stream. One Sunday I sat on the bank all day with a fishing pole and caught three tiny teaspoon-sized gudgeons—that sort of catch wouldn't fatten you up either. I didn't go there any-more—why waste the time! In the evenings I would stand around at the market near the tea room memorizing how much everything cost, practically choke on my own saliva, and go back empty-handed. There was always a hot teakettle on Aunt Nadya's stove; after warming up my stomach by slurping down some plain boiled water, I would go to bed. The next morning I'd be off to school again. That is how I held out until the joy-ous moment when the pickup arrived at the gate and Uncle Vanya knocked on the door. Half-starving and knowing that my victuals wouldn't last very long anyway no matter how I tried to ration them, I would eat my fill, stuffing my belly to the bursting point, and then, a day or two later, I'd "put my teeth on the shelf" again.

One day in September Fedka asked, "You aren't scared to play *chika*, are you?"

"What's *chika*?" I asked, not knowing what he meant.

"It's a game. You play for money. If you've got some, let's go play."

"I don't have any."

"I don't either. Let's go watch anyway. You'll see what a great game it is."

Fedka led me off beyond the gardens. We walked along the edge of a long, hunchbacked hill that was completely covered by tangled black nettles with dangling clusters of poisonous seeds. We made our way across an old dump, leaping from one trash pile to another, and down below, in a small, level empty clearing, we saw some boys. As we approached, the boys pricked up their ears. They were all about the same age I was, except for one—a strapping, muscular guy with a long tuft of red hair over his forehead whose strength and power over the others were obvious. I recognized him as a seventh-grader.

"What did you bring him for?" he asked Fedka with irritation.

"He's one of us, Vadik, one of us," Fedka tried to explain. "He lives at our house."

"You gonna play?" Vadik asked me.

"Don't have any money."

"Just make sure you don't squeal on us."

"What do you mean!" I was insulted.

They didn't pay any attention to me after that, and I stepped out of the way and began watching the game. Not everyone was playing—sometimes six played, sometimes seven, while the others only watched, rooting mainly for Vadik. He was the boss there, that I realized right away.

It took no time at all to figure out how the game was played. Each player put ten kopecks into the kitty, the pile of coins was placed tails up in the playing area—marked off by a thick line about two meters from the pot—and they'd throw a round stone called a puck from a boulder that had sunk into the ground and served as a support for the front foot. You had to throw it in such a way that it skipped as close as possible to the line without going over it—then you earned the right to hit the pot and scatter the coins first. After that you tossed the puck at the pot, trying to flip the coins so they'd land heads up. If you flipped one over, it was yours to keep, and you could throw again. If you failed, you gave the puck to the next player. But the most important thing was to cover some of the coins with the puck. If even one of them lay under the puck heads up, the whole pot went into your pocket with no argument, and the game started all over again.

Vadik was crafty. He would go up to the boulder after everyone else, when the whole pecking order was spread out before his eyes and he could see where to throw the puck to get first crack at the pot. The money usually went to the first throwers; seldom was there any left for the last ones. No doubt everyone realized what Vadik was up to, but no one dared say anything. To be sure, he was a good player in his own right. Approaching the rock, he would hunker down slightly and, narrowing his eyes, take careful aim at the target, then slowly and smoothly straighten up—the puck would slide out of his hand and fly exactly where he had aimed. With a quick movement of his head he would throw back his tousled hair, casually spit to one side, showing that he'd done a good job, and then saunter toward the money at a deliberately slow pace. If the money was in a pile, he'd strike it with a sharp, ringing bang, while individual coins he would nudge gently, bouncing the puck so that the coin would not be hit directly and fly into the air but would rise just enough to flip over to the other side. No one else could do this. The other boys threw haphazardly and then got out more coins, and the ones who had no more to get out joined the spectators.

It seemed to me that I would be able to play this game if only I had some money. In the village we had always played knucklebones, and you need a keen eye for that, too. Besides, I loved to dream up amusements for myself that required good

aim. I would gather up a handful of stones, find a difficult target, and keep throwing at it until I achieved perfect results—
ten out of ten. I could throw both overhand and underhand,
dropping the stone on the target from above. So I had a knack
for this sort of thing. What I didn't have was money.

Because our family seldom had any money, Mother sent
me bread; otherwise I would have bought my bread there in
town. And where could they have gotten money on the
kolkhoz when farmers didn't receive salaries? Nevertheless,
two or three times Mother had enclosed a five-ruble bill in her
letters—for milk. In today's terms that would be fifty
kopecks, which didn't make me rich, but it was money all the
same and just enough to buy five half-liter containers of milk
at the market for a ruble apiece. I'd been ordered to drink
milk to avoid anemia, since I was having frequent dizzy spells
for no reason.

When I received a five-ruble bill for the third time, however, I didn't go buy milk but got change for it and headed off
beyond the dump. You couldn't deny that the boys had used
their heads in choosing that spot. The clearing was surrounded
by hills and completely out of sight. In town, where the boys
could be observed, adults would get after them for playing
such games and threaten them with the school principal or the
police. There no one interfered with them. And it wasn't far
away—you could run to the clearing in ten minutes.

The first time I played, I threw away ninety kopecks—the
second time, sixty. I was sorry to lose the money, of course,
but I felt that I was acquiring the rudiments of the game and
that my hand was gradually getting used to the puck and learning how to put just the right amount of force into each throw
to make the puck go where I wanted it to. My eyes were also
learning to know in advance where the puck would land and
how much farther it would slide along the ground. In the

evening, after the other boys had all gone home, I would return, get the puck out from under the rock where Vadik had hidden it, dig the change out of my pocket, and practice throwing until it got dark. I reached the point where three or four out of every ten throws would land squarely on the money.

And finally the day arrived when I ended up a winner.

Autumn that year was warm and dry. Even as late as October you could still be outdoors without a jacket. Rain fell rarely and seemed accidental, as though driven in by a weak passing breeze from bad weather somewhere else. The sky was a summer blue, but it seemed to have shrunk, and the sun set early. When there were no clouds, the air hovered over the hills in a haze, carrying the slightly bitter, intoxicating smell of dry wormwood; distant voices could be heard clearly, along with the cries of birds heading south. The grass in our clearing, though yellowed and withered, still remained alive and soft, an ideal playground for the boys who were sitting out the game, or, to be more exact, who had already lost.

Now I ran over there every day after school. The other boys kept changing, new ones appeared, and only Vadik never missed a game. Play couldn't even begin without him. Trailing Vadik like a shadow was a stocky kid with a big shaved head whose nickname was "Birdy." I had never seen Birdy in school before, but, getting ahead of myself, I'll say that at the beginning of the third quarter he suddenly descended on our class like a bolt out of the blue. It turned out that he had to repeat fifth grade and he'd come up with some excuse for staying home until January. Birdy normally won, too, although not quite as often as Vadik, yet he never came out behind. No doubt he didn't lose anything because he was in cahoots with Vadik, and Vadik gave him a little help.

Sometimes Tishkin, another boy from our grade, would

join us in the clearing. Tishkin was a nervous kid with blinking little eyes who loved to raise his hand in class. His hand would shoot up whether he knew the answer or not. When the teachers called on him, he was silent.

"Why did you raise your hand?" they'd ask Tishkin.

He would blink his little eyes. "I had the answer, but I forgot it while I was standing up."

Tishkin and I weren't friends. My shyness, general silence, excessive rural reticence, and, most of all, uncontrollable homesickness left me with no desire whatsoever to make friends; at that time I hadn't gotten close to any of the other boys yet. They weren't drawn to me either, and I kept to myself, not able to understand my loneliness or to separate it from my wretched situation as a whole—I was alone because I was there instead of at home in the village, where I had lots of friends.

Tishkin didn't seem to notice me at all when we were in the clearing. After quickly losing his money, he would disappear and not come back to the game for a long time.

And I was winning. I started to win consistently, every day. I had my own system—you didn't necessarily have to shoot the puck across the playing surface to earn the right to throw first. That wasn't so simple when there were a lot of players, because the closer you landed to the line, the greater the danger of going over it and ending up last. You were better off covering the coins when you threw. And that is what I did. It was risky, of course, but with my skill it was worth the risk. I could lose three or four times in a row, but by winning the pot on the fifth time around, I would recoup my losses threefold. Then I would lose some and win some more back again. I rarely got the chance to knock over the coins with the puck, but when I did, I used my own method for that, too. While Vadik would bounce them back in his direction, I, on the contrary, would nudge them farther away. It was unusual, but that way the puck would hold a coin in place without letting it spin and then flip it over as it slid away.

Now I had money. I didn't let myself get too involved in the game or hang around the clearing until evening. I needed only one ruble, just one ruble a day. Once I got it, I'd run off to the market and buy a container of milk (the women there would grumble when they saw my bent, battered, worn-out coins, but they would pour milk for me anyway). Then I'd eat dinner and sit down to do my homework. I still never ate enough to get full, but the very thought that I was drinking milk gave me strength and tamed my hunger. And now my dizzy spells seemed to occur far less often.

At first Vadik reacted calmly to my winnings. He himself never lost, and my take was probably not coming out of his pocket. He even praised me on occasion by advising the other boys to learn from me: "That's the way to throw, you duffers." Vadik, however, soon noticed that I was leaving the game too quickly, and one day he stopped me.

"What are you doing? Going to grab the pot and run? What a sneak you are! Keep on playing."

"I've got homework to do, Vadik," I pleaded.

"If you've got homework, you shouldn't even come here."

Then Birdy chimed in. "Who says you can do that when you're playing for money? In case you don't know, they beat guys up for that. Got it?"

After that, Vadik never let me throw ahead of him, and he always sent me up to the rock last. He had a good throw, and quite often I reached into my pocket for another coin without even touching the puck. But my throw was better, and if I got the chance to throw, the puck would fly straight to the money like a magnet. Even I was amazed at my own accuracy. I should have thought to hold back a little, to play less conspicuously, but I naively kept on bombing away at the pot without relenting. How could I have known that no one has ever been forgiven for striving to get ahead of the pack? Don't expect any mercy then. Don't expect anyone to intercede for you, because others think you're an upstart, and the one who follows in your wake will hate you the most. This is the lesson I had to learn the hard way that autumn.

I had just landed on the money again and was about to gather it up when I noticed that Vadik was standing on one of the widely scattered coins. All the others lay tails up. In such instances you usually yelled "Pile 'em!" when you threw so that in case there wasn't a single coin heads up, the money would be gathered into one pile for another try. But I, as always, had hoped for good luck and hadn't yelled anything.

"Don't pile 'em!" Vadik decreed.

I walked up to him and tried to move his foot off the coin, but he shoved me away, quickly snatched it off the ground, and showed me tails. I'd had time to notice that the coin was heads—otherwise he wouldn't have bothered to cover it up.

"You turned it over," I said. "It was heads. I saw it."

He shoved his fist under my nose.

"Did you ever see this before? Take a whiff. What does it smell like?"

I had to give in. It was foolish to try to stand my ground. If a fight were to break out, not a soul would take my side, not even Tishkin, who was fidgeting nearby.

Vadik's sinister, narrowed eyes were staring straight at me. I crouched down, calmly hit the nearest coin, flipped it over, and nudged another one. "By hook or by crook," I decided, "I'll still win all of them right now." Once again I aimed the puck for a throw but never got it off. Suddenly someone jabbed me with a knee from behind and I clumsily keeled over onto the ground headfirst. All around me kids burst out laughing.

Birdy stood behind me, smiling expectantly. I was stunned. "Why'd you do that?!"

"Who said I did it?" he countered. "Where'd you dream that up?"

"Give it here!" Vadik said, reaching out for the puck, but I didn't hand it over. My fear was drowned out by a feeling of humiliation. Nothing on earth could have frightened me then. But why? Why were they treating me this way? What had I done to them?

"Give it here!" Vadik demanded.

"You turned the coin over!" I shouted at him. "I saw you turn it over. I saw you."

"Just say that one more time," he said while advancing toward me.

"You turned it over," I said softly, knowing full well what would happen next.

The first guy to hit me, again from behind, was Birdy. He sent me flying toward Vadik, who quickly and deftly butted his head into my face without even aiming, and I fell down with a bloody nose. No sooner had I jumped to my feet than Birdy threw himself at me again. I still could have broken loose and run, but for some reason I never gave that a thought. I was spinning between Vadik and Birdy, hardly defending myself at all, pressing a hand over my nose to try to stop the bleeding, and in despair I stubbornly kept yelling one and the same thing, which only increased their fury. "You turned it over! You turned it over! You turned it over!"

They took turns punching me, first one, then the other, then one, then the other. A third guy, small and nasty, kicked me in the legs, which were almost completely covered with bruises afterward. I just tried to stay on my feet, not to fall down no matter what, which even at that point I would have considered a disgrace. But finally they tumbled me to the ground and stopped.

"Get out of here while you're still alive!" commanded Vadik. "Get a move on!"

I got up and, sobbing and sniffling through my battered nose, dragged myself up the hill.

"Just try squealing to anybody—we'll kill you!" Vadik promised as I walked away.

I did not respond. Everything inside me had somehow closed up and hardened in humiliation, and I no longer had the strength to call up a single word.

Only when I reached the top of the hill did I let go and, like someone deranged, shout as loudly as I could, so that the whole town probably heard, "You turned it o-o-ver!"

Birdy started to chase after me, but quickly went back. Vadik evidently decided that I'd had enough and stopped him. I stood there sobbing for about five minutes and looked down at the clearing where the game had resumed, then descended the other side of the hill to the gully covered with black nettles. I fell down on the rough, dry grass, and, no longer able to hold back, I began to sob bitterly and violently.

That day there was not and could not have been anyone in the whole wide world more unhappy than I.

The next morning I looked at myself in the mirror with horror. My nose was swollen and puffed up, I had a shiner under my left eye, and just below that a fat, bloody cut wound across my cheek. How I could go to school in that condition was beyond my imagination, but I had to go anyway. I couldn't bring myself to skip classes for any reason whatsoever. Let's face it, some people are endowed by nature with noses prettier than mine, and if it weren't in its usual place, you'd never guess it was a nose at all, but there was no justification for the shiner and the cut. They quite obviously stood out through no choice of my own.

Covering my eye with one hand, I darted into the class-

room, took my seat, and put my head down on the desk. As if
to spite me, our first lesson was French. Lidia Mikhaylovna, in
her role as class supervisor, took greater interest in us than did
the other teachers, and it was difficult to conceal anything from
her. She would enter the room and greet us, but before seating
the class, she had the habit of carefully examining almost every
one of us and making suggestions that seemed humorous but
that we were obliged to follow. And of course she immediately
spotted the marks on my face despite my best attempts to hide
them. I realized this because the other kids started to turn
around and stare at me.

"Well, well," said Lidia Mikhaylovna as she opened her
record book. "Today we have some of the wounded among us."

The class burst out laughing, and Lidia Mikhaylovna lifted
her eyes in my direction again. They squinted and seemed to
look past you, but by then we had already learned to recognize
what they were looking at.

"So what happened?" she asked.

"I fell," I blurted out. For some reason I hadn't thought up
an even minimally decent explanation ahead of time.

"Oh, that's too bad. Did you fall yesterday or today?"

"Today. No, I mean last night, when it was dark."

"Fell, ha!" shouted Tishkin, choking with glee. "It was
Vadik from seventh grade who let him have it. They were playing for money, and he started arguing and got what he
deserved. I saw it. And he says he fell."

I was stunned by such treachery. Was he doing this
intentionally, or didn't he understand anything at all? Playing
for money could get you kicked out of school in a big hurry.
Now he'd done it! My head began to spin and ache from fear.
I'm sunk, now I'm sunk. Thanks, Tishkin. That's Tishkin for
you. You really did me a favor. You cleared it all up, that's for
sure.

"Tishkin, there's something else I wanted to ask you about," said Lidia Mikhaylovna, expressing no surprise and maintaining her calm, slightly indifferent tone as she interrupted him. "Go to the board, now that you're all warmed up, and get ready to recite." She waited until the distressed and suddenly unhappy Tishkin had made his way to the board and then said to me briefly, "I'd like you to stay after school."

What I feared most of all was that Lidia Mikhaylovna would drag me off to the principal's office. That meant that besides having a talk with me today, tomorrow they'd march me out in front of the school lineup and force me to explain what made me engage in this filthy business. That's how the principal, Vasily Andreevich, would question the offender no matter what he'd done wrong—broken a window, gotten into a fight, or been caught smoking in the lavatory. "What made you engage in this filthy business?" He would pace back and forth in front of the lineup with his hands behind his back, thrusting his shoulders forward in time with his long strides so that his dark, bulging, tightly buttoned field jacket seemed to move by itself a little ahead of him, and he would goad the kid, "Come on, let's have an answer. We're waiting. Look—the whole school is waiting to hear what you have to say." The pupil would begin to mumble something in his own defense, but the principal would cut him off. "Answer my question, answer my question. How did I put the question?"

"What made me do it?"

"Exactly what made you do it? We're listening."

The matter usually ended with tears, and only after that would the principal calm down, and then we would go off to our classes. This was harder on the kids in the upper grades, who didn't want to cry but still couldn't answer Vasily Andreevich's question. Once our first-hour classes started ten minutes late because all that time the principal was questioning one ninth-grader. But when he failed to get anything intelligible out of him, he led the boy away to his office.

And I wondered what I would say. Better they expel me immediately. No sooner had this thought flashed through my mind than I realized that I would then be able to go home. But I instantly got scared, as though I'd been burned. No, I certainly couldn't go home in such disgrace. It would be different if I quit school on my own . . . But even then people could say that since I hadn't passed this voluntary test, I wasn't dependable, and everyone would begin to avoid me completely. No, anything but that. I'd better endure this place a while longer, I'd better get used to it, I couldn't go home this way.

Scared stiff, I waited for Lidia Mikhaylovna in the hallway after school. She came out of the teachers' lounge and, with a nod, led me into the classroom. She sat down at her desk as always, and I started to settle into a desk in the third row some distance away, but Lidia Mikhaylovna motioned me to the first desk right in front of her.

"Is it true that you play for money?" she began at once.

She spoke too loudly. It seemed to me that in school one should talk about such things only in a whisper, and I became even more frightened. But there was no point in trying to hide anything. Tishkin had managed to betray me lock, stock, and barrel.

"Yes, it's true," I muttered.

"Well, then, how do you come out? Do you win or lose?"

I stopped short, not knowing which was better.

"Let's tell it like it is. You probably lose, right?"

"I . . . I win."

"Well, that's something. At least you win. And what do you do with the money?"

When I started school there it took me a long time to get used to Lidia Mikhaylovna's voice. It confused me. In our vil-

lage people spoke by drawing their voices up from deep down
inside, and for that reason you could hear them loud and clear,
but Lidia Mikhaylovna's voice was somehow shallow and soft
so that you had to listen to it carefully. This certainly didn't
come from feebleness—sometimes she could speak up even to
my satisfaction—but rather it seemed to come from reticence
and unnecessary economizing. I was ready to blame it all on
French. Back when she was a student and still adjusting to a
foreign tongue, her fettered voice had naturally shrunk and
grown weak, like a caged bird's. Just see if it might ever open
up and get strong again. At that moment, for instance, Lidia
Mikhaylovna was questioning me as though she were currently
preoccupied with something else, something more important,
but there was still no way to avoid answering her questions.

"Well, so what do you do with the money you win? Buy
candy? Or books? Or are you saving it up for something? You
must have a lot by now, don't you?"

"No, not much. I only win a ruble at a time."

"And then you stop playing?"

"Yes."

"Just a ruble? Why only a ruble? What do you do with it?"

"I buy milk."

"Milk?"

Seated before me, she was thoroughly tidy, intelligent,
and beautiful, beautiful in both her attire and in her feminine
youthfulness, of which I was vaguely aware. I smelled the fragrance of perfume, which I took to be her very breath. And
besides, she taught not just some ordinary subject like arith-
metic or history but the mysterious French language, which
also gave off a special fairy-tale aura that not everyone could
grasp—like me, for instance. Not daring to look her straight in
the eye, I didn't dare deceive her either. And why, after all,
should I have tried to fool her?

She paused, scrutinizing me, and I had a gut feeling that under the gaze of her squinting, penetrating eyes all my absurdities and misfortunes rose up and overflowed with all their repulsive might. I was, of course, a sight to behold. Squirming behind the desk in front of her was a skinny, uncivilized kid with a battered face, unkempt and lonely without his mother, wearing a faded old jacket with drooping shoulders that fit across the chest but left his arms hanging way out. There were traces of yesterday's fight on his easily stained, light-green pants, which had been shortened from his father's riding breeches and were now tucked into his shoes. Even before that I had noticed how quizzically Lidia Mikhaylovna would look at my footwear. I was the only kid in our whole grade who went around in such clodhoppers. Finally the next autumn, when I categorically refused to go back to school in them, Mother sold her sewing machine, the only valuable thing we had, and bought me some canvas boots.

"And yet you shouldn't play for money," Lidia Mikhaylovna said earnestly. "You should get along without that somehow. Can you?"

Still not quite believing that I had escaped punishment, I found it easy to promise.

"Yes, I can."

I spoke sincerely, but what can you do when your sincerity slips out of its moorings?

I should say in my own defense that those were very bad days for me. Because of the dry autumn, our kolkhoz had delivered its quota of grain early, and Uncle Vanya didn't come to town anymore. I knew that at home Mother was beside herself worrying about me, and that didn't make my life any easier. The sack of potatoes that Uncle Vanya had brought on his last trip had vanished as quickly as if they'd been fed to livestock, no less. It's a good thing that I had suddenly come to my senses and had thought to hide some in the abandoned shed in the back yard, because now this cache alone was keeping me alive. I would slip into the shed after school, sneaking up to it like a thief, stuff several potatoes into my pockets, and run to the end of the street and off into the hills to build a fire somewhere in a handy hidden gully. I was hungry all the time. I could feel convulsive waves rolling through my stomach even in my sleep.

In hopes of running across a new gang of players, I cautiously began to search the neighboring streets. I wandered through vacant lots and followed the kids who were drawn into the hills. But all to no avail. The season was over, and cold October winds were blowing. And only the kids in our clearing continued to gather as before. I hung around nearby and saw the puck sparkling in the sunlight, Vadik waving his arms and giving orders, and other familiar figures bending over the pot.

Finally I couldn't stand it any longer and went down to join them. I knew that I was headed for humiliation, but it was no less humiliating to accept once and for all that they had beaten me up and banished me. I was itching to see how Vadik and Birdy would react to my return and how I would handle myself. But most of all I was driven by hunger. I needed that ruble—no longer for milk but for bread. I didn't have any other way to get it.

When I approached, the game came to a stop, and all the players fixed their eyes on me. Birdy was wearing a cap with the earflaps up—it sat there casually and tauntingly, like everything else he had on—and a short-sleeved checked shirt that wasn't tucked in. Vadik was showing off in a handsome, thick zippered jacket. A bunch of quilted jackets and boys' winter coats lay nearby, thrown into one heap where a little kid of five or six sat huddled in the wind.

Birdy greeted me first. "What did you come for? Need another beating?"

"I came to play," I replied as calmly as possible while keeping an eye on Vadik.

"Who said anybody here'll play with you?" Birdy let out a curse.

"Nobody."

"What do you think, Vadik? Should we beat him up right away or wait awhile?"

"How come you're giving this guy a hard time, Birdy?" asked Vadik, narrowing his eyes at me. "You heard him. The guy came to play. Maybe he wants to win ten rubles off each of us."

"You don't even have ten rubles each," I said, just so they wouldn't think I was a coward.

"We got more than you ever dreamed of. Put your money where your mouth is, or else Birdy might really get mad. He's got a pretty hot temper."

"Should I give it to him now, Vadik?"

"Forget it. Let him play." Vadik winked at the other kids. "He plays great. We can't hold a candle to him."

This time I was a little smarter and understood what Vadik's kindness was all about. He'd evidently gotten fed up with the same dull, monotonous play, and that was why—in order to titillate his nerves and savor the taste of a real game—he decided to count me in. But as soon as I wounded his ego, they'd make me pay for it again. He'd find some reason to pick on me, and Birdy was always at his side.

I decided to play cautiously and not go for the pot. I rolled the puck just like everybody else so as not to stand out from the crowd, fearing I'd accidentally land on the money, and then I gently nudged the coins and looked back to make sure that Birdy hadn't come up from behind. For the first few days I didn't even dream of getting a ruble. Twenty or thirty kopecks, the price of a hunk of bread—that was enough. I'd take it.

But what had to happen sooner or later naturally happened. On the fourth day, when I'd won a ruble and was ready to leave, they beat me up again. To be sure, it didn't turn out too badly this time, but one trace remained—a big fat lip. In school I had to keep sucking it in. But no matter how hard I tried to conceal it, no matter how much I sucked it in, Lidia Mikhaylovna spotted it. She deliberately called me up to the board and made me read a passage of French. I couldn't have pronounced it correctly with ten healthy lips, much less with only one.

"Enough, please, enough!" Lidia Mikhaylovna looked frightened and began waving both hands to ward me off as though I were the Evil Spirit. "Just what is this, anyway? I see that I'll have to work independently with you. I have no choice."

And so began a period of awkward and agonizing days. First thing each morning, I would fearfully begin to anticipate that moment when I'd be forced to stay alone after school with Lidia Mikhaylovna and, twisting my tongue, repeat words that didn't yield to pronunciation, that were thought up just for punishment. Why else, pray tell, if not for the sake of mockery would anyone combine three vowels into one thick, elongated sound—for instance, the o in the word beaucoup (meaning "much")—it's enough to make you choke. Why force certain humming sounds through the nose when for eons it has served quite a different human need? What's the purpose? This lies beyond the bounds of reason. I would be drenched in sweat, red in the face, and gasping for breath while Lidia Mikhaylovna mercilessly and ceaselessly forced me to get callouses on my poor tongue. And why only me? There were all kinds of kids at school who spoke French no better than I did, but they were free to play and to do what they wanted while I was condemned to take the rap alone for all of them.

As it turned out, the worst was yet to come. Lidia Mikhaylovna suddenly decided that we didn't have enough time between the first and second shifts at school, and she told me to come to her apartment in the evenings. She lived right next door to the school, in the teachers' quarters. In the other, larger part of Lidia Mikhaylovna's building lived the principal himself.

Just getting there was pure torture. Already shy and reserved by nature and easily flustered over any trifle, I was literally petrified the first time I showed up at my teacher's clean, tidy apartment, afraid even to breathe. She had to tell me to take off my coat, to go into the living room, to sit down—she had to move me around like an object and practically force the words out of me. That did nothing to facilitate my progress in French. But strangely enough, we devoted even less time to the lessons there than we did at school, where the second shift supposedly interfered. Moreover, as Lidia Mikhaylovna attended to something in the apartment, she asked me personal questions or talked about herself. I suspect that she deliberately made up one story for my benefit, saying she'd majored in French only because that language had been hard for her in school and she had decided to prove to herself that she could become just as proficient as anyone else.

Seeking refuge in a corner, I kept listening for permission to go home, hoping I wouldn't have to wait long. There were lots of books in her living room. On the end table near the window stood a large, beautiful combination radio and record player—a marvelous rarity for those times and something entirely new to me. Lidia Mikhaylovna put on records, and a smooth male voice was once again teaching French. One way or another the language had me trapped. Lidia Mikhaylovna moved around the room in a simple housedress and soft felt slippers, making me shiver and shake whenever she came close to me. I just couldn't believe that I was sitting in her home. Everything there was too unusual and unexpected for me, including the very air, which was saturated with the delicate and unfamiliar smells of a life unlike the one I knew. I couldn't help but get the feeling that I was peering at that other life from the sidelines, and I felt so awkward and ashamed of myself that I hunched down even deeper into my pitiful little jacket.

Lidia Mikhaylovna was probably about twenty-five at the time. I remember her face well, with its regular and thus not terribly animated features and slightly crossed eyes, a condition she tried to conceal by squinting. I recall her tight-lipped smile that rarely widened into a grin and her coal-black hair cut short. But despite her appearance, her face displayed none of the harshness that I later noticed becomes almost a trademark with teachers as the years pass, even with those who are the kindest and gentlest by nature. But there was a cautious bewilderment mixed with a little cunning that fit her perfectly and seemed to say, "I wonder how I ended up in this place and what I'm doing here?" I now think that she must have been married at one time before I knew her. Her voice, her step— delicate but confident and relaxed—her entire manner exuded boldness and experience. And besides, I've always held the view that girls who study French or Spanish become women sooner than their classmates who study Russian, let's say, or German.

Now I'm ashamed to recall how frightened and distressed I became when Lidia Mikhaylovna, after finishing our lesson, would invite me to have supper with her. Even when I was aching with hunger, my appetite would disappear with the speed of a bullet. Sit down at the same table with Lidia

Mikhaylovna! No, no! I'd rather learn the entire French language by heart by tomorrow than come back here ever again. Even a morsel of bread would undoubtedly have gotten stuck in my throat. Apparently I'd never suspected that even Lidia Mikhaylovna ate the most ordinary food just like all of us and not some kind of manna from heaven—that's how extraordinary a person she seemed to me, how unlike all the rest.

I would jump up and, mumbling that I was full, that I didn't want anything to eat, I would back toward the door, sticking close to the wall. Lidia Mikhaylovna would look at me with astonishment and hurt feelings, but no power on earth could have stopped me. I would run out of there. This scene was repeated several times, and then Lidia Mikhaylovna, totally exasperated, stopped inviting me to her table. I breathed more freely.

One day at school I was told that a man had delivered a package for me and that it was downstairs in the cloakroom. That must have been Uncle Vanya, the truck driver from our kolkhoz—what other man could it be? The house where I lived had probably been locked, and Uncle Vanya couldn't wait around till I got home from school—that's why he'd left it in the cloakroom. I could hardly wait until the end of classes and then I raced downstairs. Auntie Vera, the school janitor, showed me the corner where they'd put the white plywood box, the kind they package things in for mailing. I was surprised. Why in a box? Mother usually sent food in an ordinary sack. Maybe it wasn't meant for me at all? No, my last name and grade were spelled out on the lid. Evidently Uncle Vanya had written them there when he got to the school, so there wouldn't be any mix-up. How had Mother ever thought of sealing up food in a box? Look how smart she'd gotten!

I couldn't carry the package home without first finding out what was inside—I was too impatient. Clearly it was not potatoes. The container was probably too small for bread and not the right shape either. Besides that, they'd just sent me bread recently, and I still had some left. Then what was in it? Right then and there, at school, I ducked under the stairs where I remembered seeing an axe, and, after finding it, I pried off the lid. It was dark under the stairs, so I crawled back out and, looking around like a thief, set the box on the nearest window ledge.

I peered into the box and was dumbfounded. On top, neatly covered with a big sheet of white paper, lay pasta. Fantastic! The long yellow tubes, arranged side by side in even rows, sparkled in the light—a treasure more sumptuous than anything I could imagine. Now I knew why Mother had used a box—so that the pasta wouldn't break or shatter, so it would reach me safe and sound. I carefully took out one tube, inspected it, blew into it, and unable to hold back any longer, began to chomp on it voraciously. Then I grabbed a second one the same way, and a third, thinking about where I might hide the box so that my pasta wouldn't get eaten by the altogether too gluttonous mice in my landlady's cupboard. That's not why Mother had bought it, why she'd spent her last savings. No, I wouldn't be that careless with pasta. This wasn't just any old sack of potatoes.

Then suddenly I came to my senses. Pasta . . . Really now, where could Mother have gotten pasta? In all my life I'd never seen any in our village. You couldn't buy it there for all the money in the world. So what was going on here? I hastily dug through the pasta in hope and despair and found several big lumps of sugar and two bars of hematogen* at the bottom of the box. The hematogen confirmed that it wasn't Mother who'd sent the package. In that case, who was it? Who? I looked at

*hematogen: A remedy for anemia consisting of hemoglobin in a base of glycerine and wine.

the lid again. Sure enough, my grade, my last name—it was for
me. Interesting, very interesting.

I tapped the nails back into the lid and, leaving the box on
the window ledge, went up to the second floor and knocked on
the door of the teachers' lounge. Lidia Mikhaylovna had
already left. Never mind, we'll find her, we know where she
lives, we've been there before. So this is what she's up to: if you
won't sit down at my table, you'll get food delivered to your
home. So that's how it is. But it won't work. It couldn't be anyone else. It definitely wasn't Mother. She wouldn't have forgotten to enclose a note, and she would have told me where she'd
gotten it, in what mines she'd dug up such a treasure.

When I squeezed sideways through her door with the
package, Lidia Mikhaylovna pretended not to understand. She
looked at the box that I set down on the floor in front of her
and asked in surprise, "What's this? What on earth did you
bring me? And for what reason?"

"You're the one who did this," I said in a shaky, stuttering
voice.

"What have I done? What are you talking about?"

"You sent this package to the school. I just know it was
you."

I noticed that Lidia Mikhaylovna was blushing and looked
embarrassed.

That was apparently the only time I had not been afraid to
look her straight in the eye. I couldn't have cared less whether
she was my teacher or a distant aunt. Now I was the one asking
the questions, not her, and I was asking them not in French but
in Russian, where I didn't have to worry about any articles. And
she had to answer.

"Why have you decided it was me?"

"Because we don't have pasta in our village. And we don't
have hematogen either."

"How can that be? You never have them?" Her astonishment was so genuine that she gave herself away completely.

"Never. You should have known that."

Lidia Mikhaylovna suddenly burst out laughing and tried to hug me, but I moved away from her.

"You're right. I really should have known. How could I have made such a mistake?" She paused for a moment, deep in thought. "But honestly, I could hardly have guessed! I'm a city girl, after all. You say you never have these things? What do you have, then?"

"We have peas. We have radishes."

"Peas . . . radishes . . . Along the Kuban River we have apples. My, how many apples there are right now! I wanted to go back to the Kuban recently, but for some reason I came here instead." Lidia Mikhaylovna sighed and glanced at me out of the corner of her eye. "Don't be angry with me. I wanted to do what was best for you. Who would have thought that I'd slip up on pasta? Never mind, I'll know better next time. But here, you take this pasta—"

"I won't take it," I interrupted.

"But why do you say that? I know you're hungry. And I live by myself. I've got lots of money. I can buy whatever I want, but living alone, you know . . . And I don't even eat very much because I'm afraid of putting on weight."

"I'm not hungry at all."

"Please don't argue with me. I know. I spoke with your landlady. What's so bad about taking this pasta now and making yourself a good dinner tonight? Why can't I help you—just once in my life? I promise not to force any more packages on you. But please take this one, for my sake. You have to eat your fill in order to study. We have a lot of well-fed goof-offs at school who can't figure out anything and undoubtedly never will, but you're an able kid. You shouldn't quit school."

Her voice was beginning to break down my resistance. I was afraid she would convince me, and, angry with myself for recognizing the validity of Lidia Mikhaylovna's arguments and for planning to reject them anyway, I shook my head, mumbled something, and ran out the door.

Our lessons didn't end with that. I continued to visit Lidia Mikhaylovna. But now she really took me in tow. She'd evidently decided, Well then, if it's just French, then let it be French. It's true that some good was coming of this. Gradually I began to enunciate French words tolerably, and they no longer broke off and fell at my feet like heavy cobblestones but tried to take wing with a lilt.

"That's good," said Lidia Mikhaylovna encouragingly. "You still won't get an A this quarter, but next quarter you will for sure."

We didn't bring up the subject of the package, but I was on my guard just in case. Lidia Mikhaylovna was capable of coming up with almost anything. I knew from my own experience that when something isn't working out, you'll do everything to make sure it does; you won't back off that easily. I had the feeling that Lidia Mikhaylovna was always sizing me up expectantly, chuckling over my primitiveness all the while. I would get angry, but my anger, however strange this may seem, helped me behave more confidently. I was no longer the meek, helpless kid who'd been scared to set foot in there. Little by little I was getting used to Lidia Mikhaylovna and her apartment. I was still bashful, of course, taking refuge in a corner, covering up my clodhoppers under the table, but my former constraint and sullenness were receding, and now I had the courage to ask Lidia Mikhaylovna questions and even to get into arguments with her.

She made one more attempt to seat me at her supper

table. But in this matter I was unbending. I had enough stub-
bornness for ten people.

We probably could have curtailed those review sessions at
her home. I had grasped the essentials, my tongue had loosened up and begun to move, and the rest would have come
with time during our regular classes. Years and years lay ahead.
What would I do later if I were to learn it all from beginning to
end in one fell swoop? But somehow I couldn't say this to Lidia
Mikhaylovna, and she evidently didn't feel that we'd achieved
our goal at all, so I kept my nose to the French grindstone. But
was it really such a grind? Somehow, without ever expecting to
and without noticing, I'd automatically developed a taste for
the language, and in my spare time I'd look things up in my little dictionary without any prodding and glance ahead at more
advanced passages in the textbook. Punishment was turning
into pleasure. I was still spurred on by pride. Where I had failed
I would succeed and succeed just as well as the very best of
them. I was cut from the same cloth, wasn't I? If I had no
longer been required to go to Lidia Mikhaylovna's, I would have
managed all by myself.

One day, about two weeks after the incident with the
package, Lidia Mikhaylovna asked with a smile, "Well, have you
given up playing for money? Or do you still get together in
some out-of-the-way spot and play now and then?"

"How could we play now?" I asked with surprise, glancing
out the window at the snow.

"And what kind of game was it? How is it played?"

"What do you care?" My guard went up.

"I'm just curious. When I was a kid we sometimes played a
game like that, too. I'd simply like to know whether yours is the
same game or not. Come on, tell me about it. Don't be afraid."

I told her all about it, leaving out, of course, the parts
about Vadik, Birdy, and the little tricks I used in the game.

"No," said Lidia Mikhaylovna, shaking her head. "We played 'hit the wall.' Do you know what that is?"

"No."

"Here, watch." She sprang up gracefully from the table she'd been sitting at, found a couple of coins in her purse, and moved a chair away from the wall. "Come here and watch. First I bounce a coin off the wall." Lidia Mikhaylovna tossed it gently, and the coin, hitting the wall with a ping, rebounded in an arc and fell to the floor. "Now"—Lidia Mikhaylovna put the other coin in my hand—"it's your turn to throw, but keep this in mind: you have to toss it so that your coin will land as close as possible to mine. So that you can measure the distance by reaching with the thumb and little finger of one hand. Another name for the game is 'measures.' If you can reach, that means you win. Go ahead and throw."

I threw, and my coin, landing on its edge, rolled off into a corner.

"Oh, no," said Lidia Mikhaylovna, dismissing my toss with a wave of her hand. "Too far. This time you start. Don't forget— if my coin touches yours even slightly, even on the edge, then I win double. Have you got it?"

"What's so hard about that?"

"Shall we play?"

I couldn't believe my ears. "How can I ever play with you?"

"And why not?"

"Because you're a teacher!"

"What's that got to do with it? Teachers are people, too, aren't they? Sometimes I get tired of being only a teacher— teach, teach, teach all day long, constantly reminding myself that I mustn't do this, I mustn't do that." Lidia Mikhaylovna narrowed her eyes even more than usual and looked out the window, lost in her own thoughts. "Occasionally it helps to forget that you're a teacher. If you don't, you become such an ogre, such a bogeyman, that real people get bored with you. Maybe the most important thing for a teacher is not to take yourself too seriously, to realize that there's actually very little you can teach." She pulled herself together and immediately became more cheerful. "At your age I was a pretty naughty little girl. My parents had their hands full with me. Even now I still often get the urge to skip and jump and race off somewhere, to do something that's not in the curriculum and not scheduled, just because I want to. Once in a while I skip and jump right here. A person gets old not when he reaches old age but when he stops being a child. I'd have a good time jumping every day if Vasily Andreevich didn't live next door. He's a very strict person. Under no circumstances should he find out that we're playing 'measures.' "

"But we're not even playing 'measures.' You only showed me how."

"We could play just for fun, as they say. But all the same, don't you tell on me."

Good Lord, what was the world coming to! Not long ago I had been scared to death that Lidia Mikhaylovna would drag me off to the principal's office because I was playing for money, and now she was asking me not to squeal on her. Doomsday had arrived—that's what it was. I looked around, afraid of who knows what, my eye blinking nervously.

"Well, what do you say? Shall we try it? If you don't like it, we'll quit."

"Okay," I agreed reluctantly.

"You start."

We grabbed our coins. I could see that Lidia Mikhaylovna had actually played before, while I was just starting to size up the game. I still hadn't figured out for myself how to bounce a coin off the wall—on its edge or flat—or how high or how hard to throw it. I was throwing blindly. If we'd been keeping score for the first few minutes, I would have lost quite a bit, although there was nothing tricky about that game called "measures." Understandably, what held me back and upset me most of all, what kept me from learning the game, was playing it with Lidia Mikhaylovna. Such a thing couldn't have happened even in my worst thoughts or wildest dreams. It took a good deal of time and effort to collect my wits, but when I did and gradually began to focus on the game, Lidia Mikhaylovna suddenly stopped it.

"No, this isn't very interesting," she said, straightening up and brushing back the hair that had fallen into her eyes. "If we're going to play, let's play for real, otherwise we're like a couple of three-year-olds."

"But that means playing for money," I reminded her shyly.

"Of course. And what do we have in our hands? There's nothing quite like playing for money. This makes it both good and bad at the same time. Even if we agree on very small stakes, it will make it interesting."

I was speechless, not knowing what to do or how to react.

"You're not scared, are you?" asked Lidia Mikhaylovna, egging me on.

"What do you mean? I'm not scared of anything."

I had a little change with me. I gave Lidia Mikhaylovna her coin back and reached into my pocket for one of my own. Okay, Lidia Mikhaylovna, let's play for real if that's what you want. What's it to me—I'm not the one who started this. Vadik didn't pay any attention to me at first either, but then he woke up and came after me with his fists. I learned that game, and I'll learn this one, too. It isn't French, and I'll even have French under my belt pretty soon.

I had to accept one condition. Since Lidia Mikhaylovna had larger hands and longer fingers, she would measure with her thumb and middle finger while I would measure with my thumb and little finger, the way you were supposed to. That was only fair, and I agreed to it.

The game began again. We moved from the living room to the entryway, where we had a little more space and could throw against the smooth, wooden room divider. We threw, got down on our knees, crawled around on the floor, bumping into each other, stretched out our fingers, measuring between the coins, then got to our feet again, and Lidia Mikhaylovna kept score. She made a lot of racket during the game. She'd let out a shout, clap her hands, and tease me all the time—in other words, she behaved like a typical little girl instead of a teacher, and sometimes I even got the urge to yell at her. But she still won, and I lost. Before I knew it, I'd blown eighty kopecks. I had a lot of trouble cutting my debt down to thirty, but then Lidia Mikhaylovna, shooting from a long way out, landed her coin on mine, and the score quickly jumped to minus fifty. I began to get worried. We had agreed to settle up at the end of the game, but if things went on this way, I would soon be out of money. I had just a little over a ruble. And so I couldn't lose more than a ruble—otherwise I'd be disgraced, disgraced and ashamed for the rest of my life.

And then I happened to notice that Lidia Mikhaylovna wasn't even trying to beat me at all. When measuring, she would bend her fingers instead of extending them to their full length—once, when she supposedly couldn't reach a coin, I reached it without any effort. That hurt my feelings, and I stood up.

"None of that," I announced. "I won't play that way. Why are you trying to let me win? That's dishonest."

"But I really can't reach them," she said, denying the accusation. "My fingers are kind of stiff."

"Yes, you can."

"All right, all right, I'll try harder."

I don't know how it is in mathematics, but in life the best proof for something lies in its opposite. The next day when I saw Lidia Mikhaylovna slyly move a coin toward her finger in order to reach it, I was dumbfounded. Glancing at me and somehow not noticing that I could see right through her obvious cheating, she continued to move the coin as though nothing were wrong.

"What are you doing?" I asked indignantly.

"Who, me? What does it look like I'm doing?"

"Why did you move the coin?"

"But I didn't. It was right here to start with," Lidia Mikhaylovna said with utter unscrupulousness and even a kind of glee, sticking to her guns just the way Vadik or Birdy would have.

That's terrific! And she calls herself a teacher! I'd seen with my own eyes from twenty centimeters away how she nudged the coin, and she tries to tell me she didn't touch it, and laughs at me to boot. Does she think I'm blind, or what? Or some little kid? And she calls herself a French teacher. In an instant I completely forgot that just the day before Lidia Mikhaylovna had been trying to let me win, and now I watched her like a hawk to make sure she didn't cheat in her own favor. What do you know about that! And she calls herself Lidia Mikhaylovna.

That day we worked on French for about fifteen or twenty minutes, and even less on the following days. We had found another common interest. Lidia Mikhaylovna would have me read a passage aloud, make corrections, and listen to me again. Then, without wasting time, we'd switch to the game. After two insignificant losses I began to win. I quickly got the hang of "measures," I fathomed all its secrets, I knew how and where to throw and what tricks to use so that Lidia Mikhaylovna wouldn't be able to reach my coin.

And once again I had money. Once again I was running to the market and buying milk—now in round, frozen chunks. I would carefully shave the layer of cream off the top, stuff the crumbling, frozen slices into my mouth, and, savoring their nourishing sweetness throughout my whole body, close my eyes with satisfaction. Then I'd turn the chunk over and use the knife to tap the slightly sweet milk solids loose. I'd let the rest melt and then drink it while eating a piece of bread.

That wasn't bad, you could stay alive that way, and in the near future, as soon as the wounds of war had healed, we were promised happier times.

Of course, I felt uncomfortable taking Lidia Mikhaylovna's money, but I consoled myself each time with the knowledge that those were honest winnings. I never asked if we could play. Lidia Mikhaylovna suggested it herself. I didn't dare refuse. The game seemed to give her a lot of pleasure—she'd become cheerful, and she'd laugh and pick on me.

If only we'd known how all this would end . . .

Kneeling across from each other, we'd gotten into an argument about the score. Just before that, as I recall, we'd been arguing about something else.

"You don't understand, you scatterbrain," contended Lidia Mikhaylovna, waving her arms as she crawled toward me. "Why would I try to cheat? I'm keeping score, not you. I know better. I lost three times in a row, and before that you won at *chika*."

"*Chika* doesn't count."

"Why doesn't it count?"

"You won at *chika*, too."

We were shouting and interrupting each other when we heard a surprised, you might even say astonished, but gruff and trembling voice.

"Lidia Mikhaylovna!"

We froze. Vasily Andreevich was standing in the doorway.

"Lidia Mikhaylovna, what's the matter with you? What's going on here?"

Lidia Mikhaylovna, beet red and all disheveled, got up from her knees very, very slowly, and, smoothing her hair, she said, "Vasily Andreevich, I would have expected you to knock before coming in."

"I did knock. No one answered. What's going on here? Please explain this. As your principal I have a right to know . . ."

"We're playing 'hit the wall,'" Lidia Mikhaylovna calmly replied.

"You're playing for money with this . . . ?" Vasily Andreevich gave me a poke with his finger, and I, terrified, crawled around the room divider to go hide in the living room. "You're playing with a pupil? Did I understand you correctly?"

"That's right."

"Don't tell me . . ." The principal was choking and gasping for air. "I'm not even sure what to call your action here. This is a crime. It's perversion. Corruption of a minor. And . . . and . . . so on . . . I've worked in schools for twenty years, I've seen all sorts of things, but this—"

And he threw up his hands.

Lidia Mikhaylovna left three days later. On the eve of her departure she met me after school and walked me home.

"I'm going back to my Kuban," she told me as we said good-bye. "And I want you to continue your studies without worrying. No one is going to lay a finger on you for this foolish incident. It's all my fault. So go on with your studies." She patted me on the head and walked away.

And I never saw her again.

In the middle of the winter, after our January break, I received a package in the mail at school. When I opened it, after getting the axe out from under the stairs again, I found sticks of pasta lying in neat, tightly packed rows. And underneath, wrapped in thick cotton wool, I found three red apples.

Until then I'd only seen pictures of apples, but I guessed that's what they were.

—TRANSLATED BY GERALD MIKKELSON
AND MARGARET WINCHELL

A GENTLEMAN'S AGREEMENT

Elizabeth Jolley

AUSTRALIA

In the home science lesson I had to unpick my darts as Mrs. Kay said they were all wrong and then I scorched the collar of my dress because I had the iron too hot. And then the sewing machine needle broke and there wasn't a spare and Mrs. Kay got really wild and Peril Page cut all the notches off her pattern by mistake and that finished everything.

"I'm not ever going back to that school," I said to Mother in the evening. "I'm finished with that place!" So that was my brother and me both leaving school before we should have and my brother kept leaving jobs too, one job after another, sometimes not even staying long enough in one place to wait for his pay.

But Mother was worrying about what to get for my brother's tea.

"What about a bit of lamb's fry and bacon," I said. She brightened up then and, as she was leaving to go up the terrace for her shopping, she said, "You can come with me tomorrow then and we'll get through the work quicker." She didn't seem to mind at all that I had left school.

Mother cleaned in a large block of luxury apartments. She had keys to the flats and she came and went as she

pleased and as her work demanded. It was while she was
working there that she had the idea of letting the people from
down our street taste the pleasures rich people took for granted in their way of living. While these people were away to
their offices or on business trips she let our poor neighbors in.
We had wedding receptions and parties in the penthouse and
the old folk came in to soak their feet and wash their clothes
while Mother was doing the cleaning. As she said, she gave a
lot of pleasure to people without doing anybody any harm,
though it was often a terrible rush for her. She could never
refuse anybody anything and, because of this, always had
more work than she could manage and more people to be kind
to than her time really allowed.

Sometimes at the weekends I went with Mother to look at
Grandpa's valley. It was quite a long bus ride. We had to get off
at the twenty-nine-mile peg, cross the Medulla brook, and walk
up a country road with scrub on either side till we came to
some cleared acres of pasture which was the beginning of her
father's land. She struggled through the wire fence hating the
mud. She wept out loud because the old man hung on to his
land and all his money was buried, as she put it, in the sodden
meadows of cape weed and stuck fast in the outcrops of granite
higher up where all the topsoil had washed away. She couldn't
sell the land because Grandpa was still alive in a Home for the
Aged, and he wanted to keep the farm though he couldn't do
anything with it. Even sheep died there. They either starved or
got drowned depending on the time of the year. It was either
drought there or flood. The weatherboard house was so neglect-
ed it was falling apart, the tenants were feckless, and if a calf
was born there it couldn't get up, that was the kind of place it
was. When we went to see Grandpa he wanted to know about
the farm and Mother tried to think of things to please him. She
didn't say the fence posts were crumbling away and that the

castor oil plants had taken over the yard so you couldn't get through to the barn.

There was an old apricot tree in the middle of the meadow, it was as big as a house and a terrible burden to us to get the fruit at just the right time. Mother liked to take some to the hospital so that Grandpa could keep up his pride and self-respect a bit.

In the full heat of the day I had to pick with an apron tied round me, it had deep pockets for the fruit. I grabbed at the green fruit when I thought Mother wasn't looking and pulled off whole branches so it wouldn't be there to be picked later.

"Don't take that branch!" Mother screamed from the ground. "Them's not ready yet. We'll have to come back tomorrow for them."

I lost my temper and pulled off the apron full of fruit and hurled it down but it stuck on a branch and hung there quite out of reach either from up the tree where I was or from the ground.

"Wait! Just you wait till I get a holt of you!" Mother pranced round the tree and I didn't come down till we had missed our bus and it was getting dark and all the dogs in the little township barked as if they were insane, the way dogs do in the country, as we walked through trying to get a lift home.

One Sunday in the winter it was very cold but Mother thought we should go all the same. We passed some sheep huddled in a natural fold of furze and withered grass all frost sparkling in the morning.

"Quick!" Mother said. "We'll grab a sheep and take a bit of wool back to Grandpa."

"But they're not our sheep," I said.

"Never mind!" And she was in among the sheep before I could stop her. The noise was terrible but she managed to grab a bit of wool.

"It's terrible dirty and shabby," she complained, pulling at the shreds with her cold fingers. "I don't think I've ever seen such miserable wool."

All that evening she was busy with the wool, she did make me laugh.

"How will modom have her hair done?" She put the wool on the kitchen table and kept walking all round it talking to it. She tried to wash it and comb it but it still looked awful so she put it round one of my curlers for the night.

"I'm really ashamed of the wool," Mother said next morning.

"But it isn't ours," I said.

"I know but I'm ashamed all the same," she said. So when we were in the penthouse at South Heights she cut a tiny piece off the bathroom mat. It was so soft and silky. And later we went to visit Grandpa. He was sitting with his poor paralyzed legs under his tartan rug.

"Here's a bit of the wool clip, Dad," Mother said, bending over to kiss him. His whole face lit up.

"That's nice of you to bring it, really nice." His old fingers stroked the little piece of nylon carpet.

"It's very good, deep and soft," he smiled at Mother.

"They do wonderful things with sheep these days, Dad," she said.

"They do indeed," he said, and all the time he was feeling the bit of carpet.

"Are you pleased, Dad?" Mother asked him anxiously. "You are pleased, aren't you?"

"Oh yes I am," he assured her.

I thought I saw a moment of disappointment in his eyes, but the eyes of old people often look full of tears.

On the way home I tripped on the steps.

"Ugh! I felt your bones!" Really Mother was so thin it hurt to fall against her.

"Well what d'you expect me to be, a boneless wonder?"

Really Mother had such a hard life and we lived in such a cramped and squalid place. She longed for better things and she needed a good rest. I wished more than anything the old man would agree to selling his land. Because he wouldn't sell I found myself wishing he would die and whoever really wants to wish someone to die! It was only that it would sort things out a bit for us.

In the supermarket Mother thought and thought what she could get for my brother for his tea. In the end all she could come up with was fish fingers and a packet of jelly beans.

"You know I never eat fish! And I haven't eaten sweets in years." My brother looked so tall in the kitchen. He lit a cigarette and slammed out and Mother was too tired and too upset to eat her own tea.

Grandpa was an old man and though his death was expected it was unexpected really and it was a shock to Mother to find she suddenly had eighty-seven acres to sell. And there was the house too. She had a terrible lot to do as she decided to sell the property herself and, at the same time, she did not want to let down the people at South Heights. There was a man interested to buy the land, Mother had kept him up her sleeve for years, ever since he had stopped once by the bottom paddock to ask if it was for sale. At the time Mother would have given her right arm to be able to sell it and she promised he should have first refusal if it ever came on the market.

We all three, Mother and myself and my brother, went out at the weekend to tidy things up. We lost my brother and then we suddenly saw him running and running and shouting, his voice lifting up in the wind as he raced up the slope of the valley.

"I do believe he's laughing! He's happy!" Mother just stared at him and she looked so happy too.

I don't think I ever saw the country look so lovely before.

The tenant was standing by the shed. The big tractor had crawled to the doorway like a sick animal and had stopped there, but in no time my brother had it going.

It seemed there was nothing my brother couldn't do. Suddenly after doing nothing in his life he was driving the tractor and making fire breaks, he started to paint the sheds and he told Mother what fencing posts and wire to order. All these things had to be done before the sale could go through. We all had a wonderful time in the country. I kept wishing we could live in the house, all at once it seemed lovely there at the top of the sunlit meadow. But I knew that however many acres you have they aren't any use unless you have money too. I think we were all thinking this but no one said anything though Mother kept looking at my brother and the change in him.

There was no problem about the price of the land, this man, he was a doctor, really wanted it and Mother really needed the money.

"You might as well come with me," Mother said to me on the day of the sale. "You can learn how business is done." So we sat in this lawyer's comfortable room and he read out from various papers and the doctor signed things and Mother signed. Suddenly she said to them, "You know my father really loved his farm but he only managed to have it late in life and then he was never able to live there because of his illness." The two men looked at her.

"I'm sure you will understand," she said to the doctor, "with your own great love of the land, my father's love for his valley. I feel if I could live there just to plant one crop and stay while it matures, my father would rest easier in his grave."

"Well I don't see why not." The doctor was really a kind man. The lawyer began to protest, he seemed quite angry.

"It's not in the agreement," he began to say. But the doctor silenced him, he got up and came round to Mother's side of the table.

"I think you should live there and plant your one crop and stay while it matures," he said to her. "It's a gentleman's agreement," he said.

"That's the best sort," Mother smiled up at him and they shook hands.

"I wish your crop well," the doctor said, still shaking her hand.

The doctor made the lawyer write out a special clause which they all signed. And then we left, everyone satisfied. Mother had never had so much money and the doctor had the valley at last but it was the gentleman's agreement which was the best part.

My brother was impatient to get on with improvements.

"There's no rush," Mother said.

"Well one crop isn't very long," he said.

"It's long enough," she said.

So we moved out to the valley and the little weatherboard cottage seemed to come to life very quickly with the pretty things we chose for the rooms.

"It's nice whichever way you look out from these little windows," Mother was saying and just then her crop arrived. The carter set down the boxes along the edge of the verandah and, when he had gone, my brother began to unfasten the hessian coverings. Inside were hundreds of seedlings in little plastic containers.

"What are they?" he asked.

"Our crop," Mother said.

"Yes I know, but what is the crop? What are these?"

"Them," said Mother, she seemed unconcerned, "oh they're a jarrah forest," she said.

"But that will take years and years to mature," he said.

"I know," Mother said. "We'll start planting tomorrow. We'll pick the best places and clear and plant as we go along."

"But what about the doctor?" I said. Somehow I could picture him pale and patient by his car out on the lonely road which went through his valley. I seemed to see him looking with longing at his paddocks and his meadows and at his slopes of scrub and bush.

"Well he can come on his land whenever he wants to and have a look at us," Mother said. "There's nothing in the gentleman's agreement to say he can't."

THE CONJUROR MADE OFF WITH THE DISH

Naguib Mahfouz

EGYPT

"The time has come for you to be useful," said my mother to me. And she slipped her hand into her pocket, saying, "Take this piaster and go off and buy some beans. Don't play on the way and keep away from the carts."

I took the dish, put on my clogs, and went out, humming a tune. Finding a crowd in front of the bean seller, I waited until I discovered a way through to the marble counter.

"A piaster's worth of beans, mister," I called out in my shrill voice.

He asked me impatiently, "Beans alone? With oil? With cooking butter?"

I did not answer, and he said roughly, "Make way for someone else."

I withdrew, overcome by embarrassment, and returned home defeated.

"Returning with the dish empty?" my mother shouted at me. "What did you do—spill the beans or lose the piaster, you naughty boy?"

"Beans alone? With oil? With cooking butter?—you didn't tell me," I protested.

"Stupid boy! What do you eat every morning?"

"I don't know."

"You good-for-nothing, ask him for beans with oil."

I went off to the man and said, "A piaster's worth of beans with oil, mister."

With a frown of impatience he asked, "Linseed oil? Vegetable oil? Olive oil?"

I was taken aback and again made no answer.

"Make way for someone else," he shouted at me.

I returned in a rage to my mother, who called out in astonishment, "You've come back empty-handed—no beans and no oil."

"Linseed oil? Vegetable oil? Olive oil? Why didn't you tell me?" I said angrily.

"Beans with oil means beans with linseed oil."

"How should I know?"

"You're a good-for-nothing, and he's a tiresome man—tell him beans with linseed oil."

I went off quickly and called out to the man while still some yards from his shop, "Beans with linseed oil, mister."

"Put the piaster on the counter," he said, plunging the ladle into the pot.

I put my hand into my pocket but did not find the piaster. I searched for it anxiously. I turned my pocket inside out but found no trace of it. The man withdrew the ladle empty, saying with disgust, "You've lost the piaster—you're not a boy to be depended on."

"I haven't lost it," I said, looking under my feet and round about me. "It was in my pocket all the time."

"Make way for someone else and stop bothering me."

I returned to my mother with an empty dish.

"Good grief, are you an idiot, boy?"

"The piaster . . ."

"What of it?"

"It's not in my pocket."

"Did you buy sweets with it?"

"I swear I didn't."

"How did you lose it?"

"I don't know."

"Do you swear by the Koran you didn't buy anything with it?"

"I swear."

"Is there a hole in your pocket?"

"No, there isn't."

"Maybe you gave it to the man the first time or the second."

"Maybe."

"Are you sure of nothing?"

"I'm hungry."

She clapped her hands together in a gesture of resignation.

"Never mind," she said. "I'll give you another piaster but I'll take it out of your money-box, and if you come back with an empty dish, I'll break your head."

I went off at a run, dreaming of a delicious breakfast. At the turning leading to the alleyway where the bean seller was, I saw a crowd of children and heard merry, festive sounds. My feet dragged as my heart was pulled toward them. At least let me have a fleeting glance. I slipped in among them and found the conjurer looking straight at me. A stupefying joy overwhelmed me; I was completely taken out of myself. With the whole of my being I became involved in the tricks of the rabbits and the eggs, and the snakes and the ropes. When the man came up to collect money, I drew back mumbling, "I haven't got any money."

He rushed at me savagely, and I escaped only with difficulty. I ran off, my back almost broken by his blow, and yet I was utterly happy as I made my way to the seller of beans.

"Beans with linseed oil for a piaster, mister," I said.

He went on looking at me without moving, so I repeated my request.

"Give me the dish," he demanded angrily.

The dish! Where was the dish? Had I dropped it while running? Had the conjurer made off with it?

"Boy, you're out of your mind!"

I retraced my steps, searching along the way for the lost dish. The place where the conjurer had been, I found empty, but the voices of children led me to him in a nearby lane. I moved around the circle. When the conjurer spotted me, he shouted out threateningly, "Pay up or you'd better scram."

"The dish!" I called out despairingly.

"What dish, you little devil?"

"Give me back the dish."

"Scram or I'll make you into food for snakes."

He had stolen the dish, yet fearfully I moved away out of sight and wept in grief. Whenever a passerby asked me why I was crying, I would reply, "The conjurer made off with the dish."

Through my misery I became aware of a voice saying, "Come along and watch!"

I looked behind me and saw a peep show had been set up. I saw dozens of children hurrying toward it and taking it in turns to stand in front of the peepholes, while the man began his tantalizing commentary to the pictures.

"There you've got the gallant knight and the most beautiful of all ladies, Zainat al-Banat."

My tears dried up, and I gazed in fascination at the box, completely forgetting the conjurer and the dish. Unable to overcome the temptation, I paid over the piaster and stood in front of the peephole next to a girl who was standing in front of the other one, and enchanting picture stories flowed across our vision. When I came back to my own world I realized I had lost both the piaster and the dish, and there was no sign of the conjurer. However, I gave no thought to the loss, so taken up was I with the pictures of chivalry, love, and deeds of daring. I forgot

my hunger. I forgot even the fear of what threatened me at
home. I took a few paces back so as to lean against the ancient
wall of what had once been a treasury and the chief cadi's seat
of office, and gave myself up wholly to my reveries. For a long
while I dreamed of chivalry, of Zainat al-Banat and the ghoul. In
my dream I spoke aloud, giving meaning to my words with gestures. Thrusting home the imaginary lance, I said, "Take that, O
ghoul, right in the heart!"

"And he raised Zainat al-Banat up behind him on the
horse," came back a gentle voice.

I looked to my right and saw the young girl who had been
beside me at the performance. She was wearing a dirty dress
and colored clogs and was playing with her long plait of hair. In
her other hand were the red-and-white sweets called "lady's
fleas," which she was leisurely sucking. We exchanged glances,
and I lost my heart to her.

"Let's sit down and rest," I said to her.

She appeared to go along with my suggestion, so I took
her by the arm and we went through the gateway of the ancient
wall and sat down on a step of its stairway that went nowhere,
a stairway that rose up until it ended in a platform behind
which there could be seen the blue sky and minarets. We sat in
silence, side by side. I pressed her hand, and we sat on in
silence, not knowing what to say. I experienced feelings that
were new, strange, and obscure. Putting my face close to hers,
I breathed in the natural smell of her hair mingled with an odor
of dust, and the fragrance of breath mixed with the aroma of
sweets. I kissed her lips. I swallowed my saliva, which had
taken on a sweetness from the dissolved "lady's fleas." I put my
arm around her, without her uttering a word, kissing her cheek
and lips. Her lips grew still as they received the kiss, then went
back to sucking at the sweets. At last she decided to get up. I
seized her arm anxiously. "Sit down," I said.

"I'm going," she replied simply.

"Where to?" I asked dejectedly.

"To the midwife Umm Ali," and she pointed to a house on the ground floor of which was a small ironing shop.

"Why?"

"To tell her to come quickly."

"Why?"

"My mother's crying in pain at home. She told me to go to the midwife Umm Ali and tell her to come along quickly."

"And you'll come back after that?"

She nodded her head in assent and went off. Her mentioning her mother reminded me of my own, and my heart missed a beat. Getting up from the ancient stairway, I made my way back home. I wept out loud, a tried method by which I would defend myself. I expected she would come to me, but she did not. I wandered from the kitchen to the bedroom but found no trace of her. Where had my mother gone? When would she return? I was fed up with being in the empty house. A good idea occurred to me. I took a dish from the kitchen and a piaster from my savings and went off immediately to the seller of beans. I found him asleep on a bench outside the shop, his face covered by his arm. The pots of beans had vanished and the long-necked bottles of oil had been put back on the shelf and the marble counter had been washed down.

"Mister," I whispered, approaching.

Hearing nothing but his snoring, I touched his shoulder. He raised his arm in alarm and looked at me through reddened eyes.

"Mister."

"What do you want?" he asked roughly, becoming aware of my presence and recognizing me.

"A piaster's worth of beans with linseed oil."

"Eh?"

"I've got the piaster and I've got the dish."

"You're crazy, boy," he shouted at me. "Get out or I'll bash your brains in."

When I did not move, he pushed me so violently I went sprawling onto my back. I got up painfully, struggling to hold back the crying that was twisting my lips. My hands were clenched, one on the dish and the other on the piaster. I threw him an angry look. I thought about returning home with my hopes dashed, but dreams of heroism and valor altered my plan of action. Resolutely I made a quick decision and with all my strength threw the dish at him. It flew through the air and struck him on the head, while I took to my heels, heedless of everything. I was convinced I had killed him, just as the knight had killed the ghoul. I did not stop running till I was near the ancient wall. Panting, I looked behind me but saw no signs of any pursuit. I stopped to get my breath, then asked myself what I should do now that the second dish was lost? Something warned me not to return home directly, and soon I had given myself over to a wave of indifference that bore me off where it willed. It meant a beating, neither more nor less, on my return, so let me put it off for a time. Here was the piaster in my hand, and I could have some sort of enjoyment with it before being punished. I decided to pretend I had forgotten I had done any-thing wrong—but where was the conjurer, where was the peep show? I looked everywhere for them to no avail.

Worn out by this fruitless searching, I went off to the ancient stairway to keep my appointment. I sat down to wait, imagining to myself the meeting. I yearned for another kiss redolent with the fragrance of sweets. I admitted to myself that the little girl had given me lovelier sensations that I had ever experienced. As I waited and dreamed, a whispering sound came from behind me. I climbed the stairs cautiously, and at the final landing I lay down flat on my face in order to see what was beyond, without anyone being able to notice me. I saw some ruins surrounded by a high wall, the last of what remained of the treasury and the chief cadi's seat of office. Directly under the stairs sat a man and a woman, and it was from them that the whispering came. The man looked like a tramp; the woman like one of those Gypsies that tend sheep. A suspicious inner voice told me that their meeting was similar to the one I had had. Their lips and the looks they exchanged spoke of this, but they showed astonishing expertise in the unimaginable things they did. My gaze became rooted upon them with curiosity, surprise, pleasure, and a certain amount of disquiet. At last they sat down side by side, neither of them taking any notice of the other. After quite a while the man said, "The money!"

"You're never satisfied," she said irritably.

Spitting on the ground, he said, "You're crazy."

"You're a thief."

He slapped her hard with the back of his hand, and she gathered up a handful of earth and threw it in his face. Then, his face soiled with dirt, he sprang at her, fastening his fingers on her windpipe, and a bitter fight ensued. In vain she gathered all her strength to escape from his grip. Her voice failed her, her eyes bulged out of their sockets, while her feet struck out at the air. In dumb terror, I stared at the scene till I saw a thread of blood trickling down from her nose. A scream escaped from my mouth. Before the man raised his head, I had crawled backward. Descending the stairs at a jump, I raced off like mad to wherever my legs might carry me. I did not stop running till I was breathless. Gasping for breath, I was quite unaware of my surroundings, but when I came to myself I found I was under a raised vault at the middle of a crossroads. I had never set foot there before and had no idea of where I was in relation to our quarter. On both sides sat sightless beggars, and crossing from all directions were people who paid attention to no one. In terror I realized I had lost my way and that countless difficulties lay in wait for me before I found my way home. Should I resort to asking one of the passersby to direct me? What, though, would happen if chance should lead me to a man like the seller of beans or the tramp of the waste plot? Would a miracle come about whereby I would see my mother approaching so that I could eagerly hurry toward her? Should I try to make my own way, wandering about till I came across some familiar landmark that would indicate the direction I should take?

I told myself that I should be resolute and make a quick decision. The day was passing, and soon mysterious darkness would descend.

—TRANSLATED BY DENYS JOHNSON-DAVIES

THE COMPOSITION

Antonio Skármeta

CHILE

On his birthday, they gave Pedro a soccer ball. Pedro complained, because he wanted one made out of white leather with black patches, just like the ones the professionals use. This yellow one made of plastic seemed too light.

"You try to make a goal with a header, and it just takes off flying like a bird, it's so light."

"So much the better," his father said. "That way you won'' scramble your brains."

And then he gestured with his fingers for Pedro to be quiet because he wanted to hear the radio. Over the last month, since the streets of Santiago had been filled with soldiers, Pedro had noticed that every night his dad would sit in his favorite easy chair, raise the antenna of the green appliance, and listen intently to news that came from far away.

Pedro asked his mother: "Why do you always listen to the radio with all that static?"

"Because what it says is interesting."

"What's it say?"

"Things about us, about our country."

"What things?"

"Things that are going on."

"And why is it so hard to hear?"

"Because the voice is coming from far away."

And Pedro sleepily looked out over the mountain range framed by his window, trying to figure out over which peak the radio voice was filtering.

In October, Pedro starred in some great neighborhood soccer games. He played in a tree-lined street, and running through the shadows in spring was almost as pleasant as swimming in the river during the summer. Pedro imagined that the rustling leaves were the sound of an enormous grandstand in some roofed stadium, applauding him when he received a precision pass from Daniel, the grocer's son, and made his way, like Simonsen, through the big kids on defense, to score a goal.

"Goal!" Pedro would shout, and he would run to hug everyone on his team, and they would pick him up and carry him like a kite or a flag. Though Pedro was already nine years old, he was the smallest kid for blocks around, so they nicknamed him "Shorty."

"Why are you so small?" they would ask him sometimes, to pester him.

"Because my dad is small and my mom is small."

"And for sure your grandpa and grandma too, because you're itty-bitty, teeny-tiny."

"I'm small, but I'm smart and quick. When I get the ball, nobody can stop me. The only quick thing you guys have is your tongue."

One day Pedro tried a quick move along the left flank, where the corner flag would be if that had been a perfect soccer field, and not a dirt street in the neighborhood. When he got to Daniel, the store owner's son, he faked a move forward with his hips, stopped the ball so it rested on his foot, lifted it over Daniel's body, who was face down in the dirt already, and made it roll softly between the stones that marked the goal.

"Goal!" Pedro shouted, and ran toward the center of the playing field, expecting a hug from his teammates. But this time no one moved. They were standing motionless, looking toward the store. A few windows opened and eyes appeared, staring at the corner as if some famous magician or the Circus of Human Eagles with its dancing elephants had just arrived. Other doors, however, had been slammed shut by an unexpected gust of wind. Then Pedro saw that Daniel's father was being dragged away by two men, while a squad of soldiers was aiming machine guns at him. When Daniel tried to approach, one of the men stopped him by putting a hand on his chest.

"Take it easy," the man yelled at him.

The store owner looked at his son.

"Take good care of the store for me."

The jeep took off, and all the mothers ran outside, grabbed their kids, and took them back inside. Pedro stood by Daniel in the middle of the dust cloud raised by the departing jeep.

"Why did they take him away?" he asked.

Daniel stuck his hands in his pockets, and at the bottom he squeezed the keys.

"My dad is a leftist," he said.

"What's that mean?"

"That he's antifascist."

Pedro had heard that word before, the nights his dad spent next to the green radio, but he didn't know what it meant, and most of all, it was hard for him to pronounce. The "f" and the "s" rolled around on his tongue, and when he said it, a sound full of air and saliva came out.

"What does anti-fa-fascist mean?" he asked.

His friend looked at the long, empty street and told him, as if in secret:

"That they want our country to be free. For Pinochet to leave Chile."

"And for that they get arrested?"

"I think so."

"What are you going to do?"

"I don't know."

A worker came slowly toward Daniel and ran a hand through his hair, leaving it more mussed than ever.

"I'll help you close up," he said.

Pedro headed home kicking the ball, and since there was no one in the street to play with, he ran toward the next corner to wait for the bus that would bring his father home from work. When he arrived, Pedro hugged him around the waist and his father bent over to give him a kiss.

"Hasn't your mother come home yet?"

"No," the boy said.

"Did you play a lot of soccer?"

"A little."

He felt his father's hand take his head and hug it against his jacket.

"Some soldiers came and took Daniel's dad prisoner."

"Yes, I know," his father said.

"How did you know that?"

"They called me."

"Daniel is in charge of the store now. Maybe now he'll give me candy."

"I don't think so."

"They took him away in a jeep. Like the ones you see in the movies."

His father said nothing. He breathed deeply and stood looking sadly down the street for a long time. In spite of its being daylight and springtime, only men returning slowly from work were out in the street.

"Do you think it will be on TV?"

"What?" his father asked.

"Don Daniel."

"No."

That night the three of them sat down to dinner, and although no one told him to be quiet, Pedro didn't say a word, as if infected by the silence with which his parents were eating, looking at the designs on the tablecloth as if the embroidered flowers were in some far-off place. Suddenly his mother started to cry, without making a sound.

"Why's Mom crying?"

His dad first looked at Pedro, and then at her, and didn't answer. His mother said:

"I'm not crying."

"Did someone do something to you?" Pedro asked.

"No," she said.

They finished dinner in silence, and Pedro went to put on his pyjamas, which were orange, with a lot of drawings of birds and rabbits. When he came back, his mother and father were sitting on the sofa with their arms around each other, and with their ears very close to the radio, which was giving off strange sounds, made more confusing than ever by the low volume. As if guessing that his father would put his finger to his mouth and gesture for him to be quiet, Pedro quickly asked:

"Dad, are you a leftist?"

The man looked at his son, and then at his wife, and immediately both looked at him. Then he nodded his head slowly up and down, in assent.

"Are they going to take you prisoner, too?"

"No," his father said.

"How do you know?"

"You bring me good luck, kid," the man said smiling.

Pedro leaned on the doorjamb, pleased that they weren't sending him directly to bed, like other times. He paid attention to the radio, trying to figure out what it was that drew his parents to it every night. When the voice on the radio said "the fascist junta," Pedro felt that all the things that were rolling around in his head came together, just like when one at a time the pieces of a jigsaw puzzle fit together into the figure of a sailing ship.

"Dad!" he exclaimed then. "Am I antifascist, too?"

His father looked at his wife as if the answer to that question were written in her eyes, and his mother scratched her cheek with an amused look until she said:

"You just can't tell."

"Why not?"

"Children aren't anti-anything. Children are simply children. Children your age have to go to school, study a lot, play hard, and be kind to their parents."

The next day, Pedro ate a couple of French rolls with jelly, got one finger wet in the sink, wiped the sleep out of his eyes, and took off on the fly to school so they wouldn't mark him tardy again. On the way, he found a kite tangled in the branches of a tree, but no matter how much he jumped and jumped, there was no way.

The bell hadn't stopped ringing when the teacher walked in very stiff, accompanied by a man in a military uniform, with a medal as long as a carrot on his chest, a gray moustache, and sunglasses blacker than the dirt on your knee. He didn't take them off, maybe because the sun was coming in the room like it was trying to set it on fire.

The teacher said:

"Stand up, children, and very straight."

The children got up and waited to hear from the officer, who was smiling with his toothbrush moustache below his dark glasses.

"Good morning, my little friends," he said. "I am Captain Romo, and I have come on behalf of the government, that is to say, on behalf of General Pinochet, to invite all the children from all the classes in this school to write a composition. The one who writes the nicest composition of all will receive personally from General Pinochet a gold medal and a ribbon like this one with the colors of the Chilean flag."

He put his hands behind his back, jumped to spread his legs, and stretched his neck out, raising his chin slightly.

"Attention! Be seated!"

The children obeyed, scratching themselves as if they didn't have enough hands.

"All right," the officer said, "take out your notebooks. . . . Notebooks ready? Good! Take out a pencil. . . . Pencils ready? Write this down! Title of the composition: 'My home and my family.' Understood? In other words, what you and your parents do from the time you get home from school and work. The friends who come over. What you talk about. Comments when watching TV. Whatever occurs to you with complete freedom. Ready? One, two, three: let's begin!"

"Can we erase, sir?" one boy asked.

"Yes," said the captain.

"Can we write with a Bic pen?"

"Yes, young man, of course!"

"Can we do it on graph paper, sir?"

"Certainly."

"How much are we supposed to write, sir?"

"Two or three pages."

The children raised a chorus of complaint.

"All right, then, one or two. Let's get to work!"

The children stuck their pencils between their teeth and began looking at the ceiling to see if inspiration would descend on them through some hole. Pedro was sucking and sucking on his pencil, but he couldn't get a single word out of it. He picked his nose and stuck a booger that happened to come out on the underside of his desk. Leiva, his deskmate, was chewing off his fingernails one by one.

"Do you eat them?" Pedro asked him.

"What?" his friend said.

"Your fingernails."

"No. I bite them off with my teeth, and then I spit them out. Like this. See?"

The captain approached down the aisle, and Pedro could see his hard, gilded belt buckle from just inches away.

"And aren't you working?"

"Yes, sir," Leiva said, and as fast as he could, he furrowed his brow, stuck his tongue between his teeth and put down a big "A" to start his composition. When the captain went toward the blackboard to talk with the teacher, Pedro peeked at Leiva's paper.

"What are you going to put down?"

"Whatever. And you?"

"I don't know."

"What did your folks do yesterday?"

"The same old thing. They came home, ate, listened to the radio, and went to bed."

"That's just what my mom did."

"My mom started to cry all of a sudden."

"Women go around crying all the time, didn't you ever notice?"

"I try not to cry ever. I haven't cried for over a year."

"And if I beat the shit out of you?"

"What for, if I'm your friend?"

"That's true."

The two stuck their pencils in their mouths and stared and stared up at an unlit bulb and the shadows on the walls, and their heads felt as empty as their piggy banks and as dark as a blackboard. Pedro put his mouth close to Leiva's ear and said:

"Listen, Skinny, are you antifascist?"

Leiva kept an eye on the captain. He gestured for Pedro to turn his head, and said, breathing into his ear:

"Of course, you dumb shit!"

Pedro scooted away a little bit and winked at him, just like the cowboys in the movies. Then he leaned toward his friend again, pretending to write on the blank paper:

"But you're just a kid!"

"That doesn't matter!"

"My mom told me that kids . . ."

"That's what they always say. . . . They arrested my dad and took him north."

"They did that to Don Daniel, too."

"I don't know him."

"The store owner."

Pedro looked at the blank page, and read his own hand-writing:

"What My Family Does at Night," by Pedro Malbran, Syria School, Third Grade-A.

"Skinny," he said to Leiva, "I'm going to try for the medal."

"Go for it, man!"

"If I win, I'll sell it and buy a professional-size white leather soccer ball, with black patches."

"That's if you win."

Pedro wet the end of his pencil with a little spit, sighed deeply, and started writing without interruption.

A week went by, during which one of the trees in the neighborhood fell over just from old age, a kid's bike was stolen, the garbage man didn't come by for five days, and flies blundered into people's faces, and even got into their noses, Gustavo Martínez, from across the street, got married, and they gave big pieces of cake to the neighbors. The jeep came back and carried off Professor Manuel Pedraza under arrest, the priest refused to say Mass on Sunday, Colo Colo won an international match by a huge score, and the school's white wall had a red word spread across it: "Resistance." Daniel got back to playing soccer and made one goal *de chileno* and another *de palomita*, the price of ice cream cones went up, and, on her eighth birthday, Matilde Schepp asked Pedro to kiss her on the mouth.

"You must be nuts!" he responded.

After that week, still another went by, and one day the captain came back with an armful of papers, a bag of candy and a calendar with the picture of a general.

"My dear little friends," he said to the class, "your compositions are very nice and the armed forces have been very pleased with them. On behalf of my colleagues and of General Pinochet I must congratulate you very sincerely. The gold medal didn't come to this class, but to another, somebody else got it. But to reward your nice work, I'm going to give each one of you a piece of candy, your composition with a note on it, and this calendar with a picture of our illustrious leader on it."

Pedro ate his candy on the bus, on the way home. He stood on the corner waiting for his father to get home, and later, he put his composition on the dining room table. At the bottom, the captain had written in green ink: "Bravo! Congratulations!" Stirring at his soup with a spoon in one hand, and scratching his belly with the other, Pedro waited for his father to finish reading it. His father handed the composition to his wife, and looked at her without saying anything. He started on his plate and didn't stop until he had eaten the last noodle, but without taking his eyes off her.

The woman read:

> *When my dad gits home from work, I go*
> *wait for him at the bus stop. Sometimes my mom*
> *is in the house and when my dad comes in, she*

*says to him hi, how'd it go today? Okay, my dad
says, and how did it go for you? Okay, my mom
says back. Then I go out and play soccer, and I like
to try to make goals with headers. Daniel likes to
play goalie and I get him all worked up because he
can't intercept me when I spike one at him. Then
my mom comes and says it's time to eat, Pedro,
and we sit down to eat, and I always eat everything except the beans, which I can't stand.
Afterwards, my dad and mom sit on the sofa in
the living room and play chess, and I do my homework. And after that we all go to bed, and I try to
tickle their feet. And after that, way after that, I
can't tell any more because I fall asleep.*

Signed: Pedro Malbran
*P.S. If you give me a prize for my composition, I
hope it's a soccer ball, but not a plastic one.*

"Well," his dad said, "we'll have to buy a chess set, just in
case."

—TRANSLATED BY DONALD L. SCHMIDT
AND FEDERICO CORDOVEZ

THE LADDER

V. S. Pritchett

ENGLAND

"We had the builders in at the time," my father says in his accurate way, if he ever mentions his second marriage, the one that so quickly went wrong. "And," he says, clearing a small apology from his throat as though preparing to say something immodest, "we happened to be without stairs."

It is true. I remember that summer. I was fifteen years old. I came home from school at the end of the term, and when I got to our place not only had my mother gone but the stairs had gone too. There was no staircase in the house.

We lived in an old crab-colored cottage, with long windows under the eaves that looked like eyes half-closed against the sun. Now when I got out of the car I saw scaffolding over the front door and two heaps of sand and mortar on the crazy paving, which my father asked me not to tread in because it would "make work for Janey." (This was the name of his second wife.) I went inside. Imagine my astonishment. The little hall had vanished, the ceiling had gone; you could see up to the roof; the wall on one side had been stripped to the brick, and on the other hung a long curtain of builder's sheets. "Where are the stairs?" I said. "What have you done with the stairs?" I was at the laughing age.

A mild, trim voice spoke above our heads.

"Ah, I know that laugh," the voice said sweetly and archly. There was Miss Richards, or I should say my father's second wife, standing behind a builder's rope on what used to be the landing, which now stuck out precariously without banisters, like the portion of a ship's deck. The floor appeared to have been sawn off. She used to be my father's secretary and I had often seen her in my father's office; but now she had changed. Her fair hair was fluffed out and she wore a fussed and shiny brown dress that was quite unsuitable for the country.

I remember how odd they both looked, she up above and my father down below, and both apologizing to me. The builders had taken the old staircase out two days before, they said, and had promised to put the new one in against the far wall of the room behind the dust sheets before I got back from school. But they had not kept their promise.

"We go up," said my father, cutting his wife short, for she was apologizing too much, "by the ladder."

He pointed. At that moment his wife was stepping to the end of the landing where a short ladder, with a post to hold on to at the top as one stepped on the first rung, sloped eight or nine feet to the ground.

"It's horrible," called my stepmother.

My father and I watched her come down. She came to the post and turned round, not sure whether she ought to come down the ladder frontwards or backwards.

"Back," called my father.

"No, the other hand on the post," he said.

My stepmother blushed fondly and gave him a look of fear. She put one foot on the step and then took her foot back and put the other one there and then pouted. It was only eight feet from the ground: at school we climbed halfway up the gym walls on the bars. I remembered her as a quick and practical woman at the office; she was now, I was sure, playing at being weak and dependent.

"My hands," she said, looking at the dust on her fingers as she grasped the top step.

My father and I stopped where we were and watched her. She put one leg out too high, as if, artlessly, to show the leg first. She was a plain woman and her legs (she used to say) were her "nicest thing." This was the only coquetry she had. She looked like one of those insects that try the air around them with their feelers before they move. I was surprised that my father (who had always been so polite and grave-mannered to my mother, and had almost bowed to me when he had met me at the station and helped me in and out of the car) did not go to help her. I saw an expression of obstinacy on his face.

"You're at the bottom," he said. "Only two more steps."

"Oh dear," said my stepmother, at last getting off the last step on to the floor; and she turned with her small chin raised, offering us her helplessness for admiration. She came to me and kissed me and said:

"Doesn't she look lovely? You are growing into a woman."

"Nonsense," said my father. And, in fear of being a woman and yet pleased by what she said, I took my father's arm.

"Is that what we have to do? Is that how we get to bed?" I said.

"It's only until Monday," my father said again.

They both of them looked ashamed, as though by having the stairs removed they had done something foolish. My father tried to conceal this by an air of modest importance. They seemed a very modest couple. Both of them looked shorter to me since their marriage: I was very shocked by this. *She* seemed to have made him shorter. I had always thought of my father as a dark, vain, terse man, very logical and never giving in to anyone. He seemed much less important now his secretary was in the house.

"It is easy," I said, and I went to the ladder and was up it in a moment.

"Mind," called my stepmother.

But in a moment I was down again, laughing. When I was coming down I heard my stepmother say quietly to my father, "What legs! She is growing."

My legs and my laugh: I did not think that my father's secretary had the right to say anything about me. She was not my mother.

After this my father took me round the house. I looked behind me once or twice as I walked. On one of my shoes was some of the sand he had warned me about. I don't know how it got on my shoes. It was funny seeing this one sandy footmark making work for Janey wherever I went.

My father took me through the dust curtains into the dining-room and then to the far wall where the staircase was going to be.

"Why have you done it?" I said.

He and I were alone.

"The house has wanted it for years," he said. "It ought to have been done years ago."

I did not say anything. When my mother was here, she was always complaining about the house, saying it was poky, barbarous—I can hear her voice now saying "barbarous" as if it were the name of some terrifying and savage queen—and my father had always refused to alter anything. Barbarous: I used to think of that word as my mother's name.

"Does Janey like it?" I said.

My father hardened at this question. He seemed to be saying, "What has it got to do with Janey?" But what he said was—and he spoke with amusement, with a look of quiet scorn:

"She liked it as it was."

"I did too," I said.

I then saw—but no, I did not really understand this at the time; it is something I understand now I am older—that my father was not altering the house for Janey's sake. She hated the whole place because my mother had been there, but was too tired by her earlier life in his office, fifteen years of it, too unsure of herself, to say anything. My father was making an act of amends to my mother. He was punishing Janey by "getting in builders" and making everyone uncomfortable and miserable; he was making an emotional scene with himself. He was annoying Janey with what my mother had so maddeningly wanted and which he would not give her.

After he had shown me the house, I said I would go and see Janey getting lunch ready.

"I shouldn't do that," said my father. "It will delay her. Lunch is just ready."

"Or should be," he said, looking at his watch.

We went to the sitting-room, and while we waited I sat in the green chair and he asked me questions about school and we went on to talk about the holidays. But when I answered I could see he was not listening to me but trying to catch sounds of Janey moving in the kitchen. Occasionally there were sounds: something gave an explosive fizz in a hot pan, and a saucepan lid fell. This made a loud noise and the lid spun a long time on the stone floor. The sound stopped our talk.

"Janey is not used to the kitchen," said my father.

I smiled very close to my lips, I did not want my father to see it, but he looked at me and he smiled by accident too. There was understanding between us.

"I will go and see," I said.

He raised his hand to stop me, but I went.

It was natural. For fifteen years Janey had been my

father's secretary. She had worked in an office. I remember when I went there when I was young she used to come into the room with an earnest air, leaning her head a little sideways and turning three-quarter-face to my father at his desk, leaning forward to guess at what he wanted. I admired the great knowledge she had of his affairs, the way she carried letters, how quickly she picked up the telephone if it rang, the authority of her voice. Her strength was that she had been impersonal. She had lost that strength in her marriage. As his wife, she had no behavior. When we were talking she raised her low bosom, which had become round and ducklike, with a sigh and smiled at my father with a tentative, expectant fondness. After fifteen years, a life had ended: she was resting.

But Janey had not lost her office behavior: that she now kept for the kitchen. The moment I went to the kitchen, I saw her walking to the stove where the saucepans were throbbing too hard. She was walking exactly as she had walked towards my father at his desk. The stove had taken my father's place. She went up to it with impersonal inquiry, as if to anticipate what it wanted, she appeared to be offering a pile of plates to be warmed as if they were a pile of letters. She seemed baffled because the stove could not speak. When one of the saucepans boiled over she ran to it and lifted it off, suddenly and too high, with her telephone movement: the water spilled at one. On the table beside the stove were basins and pans she was using, and she had them all spread out in an orderly way like typing; she went from one to the other with the careful look of inquiry she used to give to the things she was filing. It was not a method suitable to work in a kitchen.

When I came in, she put down the pan she was holding and stopped everything—as she would have done in the office—to talk to me about what she was doing. She was very nice about my hair, which I had had cut last term; it made me look older and I liked it better. But blue smoke rose behind her as we talked. She did not notice it.

I went back to my father.

"I didn't want to be in the way," I said.

"Extraordinary," he said, looking at his watch. "I must just go and hurry Janey up."

He was astonished that a woman so brisk in an office should be languid and dependent in a house.

"She is just bringing it in," I said. "The potatoes are ready. They are on the table. I saw them."

"On the table?" he said. "Getting cold?"

"On the kitchen table," I said.

"That doesn't prevent them being cold," he said. My father was a sarcastic man.

I walked about the room humming. My father's exasperation did not last; it gave way to a new thing in his voice. Resignation.

"We will wait if you do not mind," he said to me. "Janey is slow. And by the way," he said, lowering his voice a little, "I shouldn't mention we passed the Leonards in the road when I brought you up from the station."

I was surprised.

"Not the Leonards?" I said.

"They were friends of your mother's," he said. "You are old enough to understand. One has to be sometimes a little tactful. Janey sometimes feels . . ."

I looked at my father. He had altered in many ways. When he gave me this secret his small, brown eyes gave a brilliant flash and I opened my blue eyes very wide to receive it. He had changed. His rough black hair was clipped closer at the ears and he had that too young look which middle-aged men sometimes have, for by certain lines it can be seen that they are not as young as their faces. Marks like the minutes on the face of a clock showed at the corners of his eyes, his nose, his mouth; he was much thinner; his face had hardened. He had often been angry and sarcastic, sulking and abrupt, when my mother was with us; I had never seen him before, as he was now, blank-faced, ironical, and set in impatient boredom. After he spoke, he had actually been hissing a tune privately through his teeth at the corner of his mouth. At this moment Janey came in with a smile but without dishes, and said lunch was ready.

"Oh," I laughed when we got into the dining-room. "It is like . . . it is like France."

"France?" they both said together, smiling at me.

"Like when we all went to France before the war and you took the car," I said. I had chosen France because that seemed as far as I could get from the Leonards.

"What on earth are you talking about?" said my father, looking embarrassed. "You were only five before the war."

"I remember every bit of it. You and Mummy on the boat."

"Yes, yes," said my stepmother with melancholy importance. "I got the tickets for you all."

My father looked as though he was going to hit me. Then he gave a tolerant laugh across the table to my stepmother.

"I remember perfectly well," she said. "I'm afraid I couldn't get the peas to boil. Oh, I've forgotten the potatoes."

"Fetch them," my father said to me.

I thought she was going to cry. When I came back, I could see she *had* been crying. She was one of those very fair women in whom even three or four tears bring pink to the nose. My father had said something sharply to her, for his face was shut and hard and she was leaning over the dishes, a spoon in her hand, to conceal a wound.

After lunch I took my case and went up the ladder. It was not easy to go up carrying a suitcase, but I enjoyed it. I wished we could always have a ladder in the house. It was like being on a ship. I stood at the top thinking of my mother leaning on the rail of the ship with her new husband, going to America. I was glad she had gone because, sometimes, she sent me lovely things.

Then I went to my room and I unpacked my case. At the bottom, when I took my pyjamas out—they were the last thing—there was the photograph of my mother face downwards where it had been lying all the term. I forgot to say that I had been in trouble the last week at school. I don't know why. I was longing to be home. I felt I had to *do* something. One afternoon I went into the rooms in our passage when no one was there, and I put the snap of Kitty's father into Mary's room—I took it out of the frame—and I put Mary's brother into Olga's, and I took Maeve's mother and put her into the silver frame where Jessie's mother was: that photograph was too big and I bent the mount all the way down to get it in. Maeve cried and reported me to Miss Compton. "It was only a joke," I said. "A joke in very poor taste," Miss Compton said to me in *her* voice. "How would you like it if anyone took the photograph of your mother?" "I haven't got one," I said. Well, it was not a lie. Everyone wanted to know why I had an empty frame on my chest of drawers. I had punished my mother by leaving her photograph in my trunk.

But now the punishment was over. I took out her picture and put it in the frame on my chest, and every time I bent up from the drawers I looked at her, then at myself in the mirror. In the middle of this my stepmother came in to ask if she could help me.

"You are getting very pretty," she said. I hated her for admiring me.

I do not deny it: I hated her. She was a foolish woman. She either behaved as if the house, my father, and myself were too much hers, or as if she were an outsider. Most of the time she sat there like a visitor, waiting for attention.

I thought to myself: There is my mother, thousands of miles away, leaving us to this and treating us like dirt, and we are left with Miss Richards, of all people.

That night after I had gone to bed I heard my father and my stepmother having a quarrel. "It is perfectly natural," I heard my father say, "for the child to have a photograph of her mother."

A door closed. Someone was wandering about in the passage. When they had gone I opened my door and crept out barefoot to listen. Every step I made seemed to start a loud creak in the boards and I was so concerned with this that I did not notice I had walked to the edge of the landing. The rope was there, but in the dark I could not see it. I knew I was on the edge of the drop into the hall and that with one more step I would have gone through. I went back to my room, feeling sick. And then the thought struck me—and I could not get it out of my head all night; I dreamed it, I tried not to dream it, I turned on the light, but I dreamed it again—that Miss Richards fell over the edge of the landing. I was very glad when the morning came.

The moment I was downstairs I laughed at myself. The drop was only eight or nine feet. Anyone could jump it. I worked out how I would land on my feet if I were to jump there. I moved the ladder, it was not heavy to lift, to see what you would feel like if there were no ladder there and the house was on fire and you had to jump. To make amends for my wicked dreams in the night I saw myself rescuing Miss Richards (I should say my stepmother) as flames teased her to the edge.

My father came out of his room and saw me standing there.

"What are you pulling such faces for?" he said. And he imitated my expressions.

"I was thinking," I said, "of Miss Compton at our school."

He had not foreseen the change in Miss Richards; how she would sit in the house in her best clothes, like a visitor, expectant, forgetful, stunned by leisure, watchful, wronged, and jealous to the point of tears.

Perhaps if the builders had come, as they had promised, on the Monday, my stepmother's story would have been different.

"I am so sorry we are in such a mess," she said to me many times, as if she thought I regarded the ladder as her failure.

"It's fun," I said. "It's like being on a ship."

"You keep on saying that," my stepmother said, looking at me in a very worried way, as if trying to work out the hidden meaning of my remark. "You've never been on a ship."

"To France," I said. "When I was a child."

"Oh yes, you told me," said my stepmother.

Life had become so dull for my father that he liked having the ladder in the house.

"I hate it," said my stepmother to both of us, getting up. It is always surprising when a prosaic person becomes angry.

"Do leave us alone," my father said.

There was a small scene after this. My father did not mean by "us" himself and me, as she chose to think; he was simply speaking of himself, and he had spoken very mildly. My stepmother marched out of the room. Presently we heard her upstairs. She must have been very upset to have faced going up the ladder.

"Come on," said my father. "I suppose there's nothing for it. I'll get the car out. We will go to the builder's."

He called up to her that we were going.

Oh, it was a terrible holiday. When I grew up and was myself married, my father said: "It was a very difficult summer. You didn't realize. You were only a schoolgirl. It was a mistake." And then he corrected himself. I mean that: my father

was always making himself more correct: it was his chief vani-
ty that he understood his own behavior.

"I happened," he said—this was the correction— "to make
a very foolish mistake." Whenever he used the phrase "I happened" my father's face seemed to dry up and become distant:
he was congratulating himself. Not on the mistake, of course,
but on being the first to put his finger on it. "I happen to know
. . . I happen to have seen . . ."—it was this incidental rightness,
the footnote of inside knowledge on innumerable minor issues,
and his fatal wrongness in a large, obstinate, principled way
about anything important, which, I think, made my beautiful
and dishonest mother leave him. She was a tall woman, taller
than he, with the eyes of a cat, shrugging her shoulders, curv-
ing her long graceful back to be stroked and with a wide, champagne laugh. My father had a clipped-back monkeyish appearance and that faint grin of the bounder one sees in the hard-
looking monkeys that are without melancholy or sensibility;
this had attracted my mother, but very soon his youthful
bounce gave place to a kind of meddling honesty, and she
found him dull. And, of course, ruthless. The promptness of his
second marriage, perhaps, was to teach her a lesson. I imagine
him putting his divorce papers away one evening at his office
and realizing, when Miss Richards came in to ask if "there is
anything more tonight," that there was a woman who was reli-
able, trained, and, like himself, "happened" to have a lot of
inside knowledge.

To get out of the house with my father, to be alone with
him: my heart came alive. It seemed to me that this house was
not my home any more. If only we could go away, he and I; the
country outside seemed to me far more like home than this
grotesque divorced house. I stood longing for my stepmother
not to answer, dreading that she would come down.

My father was not a man to beg a woman to change her

mind. He went out to the garage. My fear of her coming made me stay for a moment. And then (I do not know how the thought came into my head) I went to the ladder and I lifted it away. It was easy to move a short distance, but it began to swing when I tried to put it down. I was afraid it would crash, so I turned it over and over against the other wall, out of reach. Breathlessly, I left the house.

"You have got white on your tunic," said my father as we drove off. "What have you been doing?"

"I rubbed against something," I said.

"Oh, how I love motoring," I laughed beside my father.

"Oh, look at those lovely little rabbits," I said.

"Their little white tails," I laughed.

We passed some hurdles in a field.

"Jumps," I laughed. "I wish I had a pony."

And then my terrible dreams came back to me. I was frightened. I tried to think of something else, but I could not. I could only see my stepmother on the edge of the landing. I could only hear her giving a scream and going over head first. We got into the town and I felt sick. We arrived at the builder's and my father stopped there. Only a girl was in the office, and I heard my father say in his coldest voice, "I happen to have an appointment . . ."

My father came out, and we drove off. He was cross.

"Where are we going?" I said, when I saw we were not going home.

"To Longwood," he said. "They're working over there." I thought I would faint.

"I—I . . ." I began.

"What?" my father said.

I could not speak. I began to get red and hot. And then I remembered. "I can pray."

It is seven miles to Longwood. My father was a man who

enjoyed talking to builders; he planned and replanned with them, built imaginary houses, talked about people. Builders have a large acquaintance with the way people live; my father liked inside knowledge, as I have said. Well, I thought, she is over. She is dead by now. I saw visits to the hospital. I saw my trial.

"She is like you," said the builder, nodding to me. All my life I shall remember his moustache.

"She is like my wife," said my father. "My first wife. I happen to have married again."

(He liked puzzling and embarrassing people.)

"Do you happen to know a tea place near here?" he said.

"Oh no," I said. "I don't feel hungry."

But we had tea at Gilling. The river is across the road from the tea-shop and we stood afterwards on the bridge. I surprised my father by climbing the parapet.

"If you jumped," I said to my father, "would you hurt?"

"You'd break your legs," said my father.

Her "nicest thing"!

I shall not describe our drive back to the house, but my father did say, "Janey will be worried. We've been nearly three hours. I'll put the car in afterwards."

When we got back, he got out quickly and went down the path. I got out slowly. It is a long path leading across a small lawn, then between two lime trees; there are a few steps down where the roses are, and across another piece of grass you are at the door. I stopped to listen to the bees in the limes, but I could not wait any longer. I went into the house.

There was my stepmother standing on the landing above the hall. Her face was dark red, her eyes were long and violent, her dress was dirty and her hands were black with dust. She had just finished screaming something at my father and her mouth had stayed open after her scream. I thought I could *smell* her anger and her fear the moment I came into the house, but it was really the smell of a burned-out saucepan coming from the kitchen.

"You moved the ladder! Six hours I've been up here. The telephone has been ringing, something has burned on the stove. I might have burned to death. Get me down, get me down. I might have killed myself. Get me down," she cried, and she came to the gap where the ladder ought to have been.

"Don't be silly, Janey," said my father. "I didn't move the ladder. Don't be such a fool. You're still alive."

"Get me down," Janey cried out. "You liar, you liar, you liar. You did move it."

My father lifted the ladder, and as he did so he said:

"The builder must have been."

"No one has been," screamed my stepmother. "I've been alone. Up here!"

"Daddy isn't a liar," I said, taking my father's arm.

"Come down," said my father when he had got the ladder in place. "I'm holding it."

And he went up a step or two towards her.

"No," shrieked Janey, coming to the edge.

"Now, come on. Calm yourself," said my father.

"No, no, I tell you," said Janey.

"All right, you must stay," said my father, and stepped down.

That brought her, of course.

"*I* moved the ladder," I said when she came down.

"Oh," said Janey, swinging her arm to hit me, but she fainted instead.

That night my father came to my room when I was in bed. I had moved my mother's photograph to the bedside table. He was not angry. He was tired out.

"Why did you do it?" he asked.

I did not answer.

"Did you know she was upstairs?" he said.

I did not reply.

"Stop playing with the sheet," he said. "Look at me. Did you know she was upstairs?"

"Yes," I said.

"You little cat," he said.

I smiled.

"It was very wrong," he said.

I smiled. Presently he smiled. I laughed.

"It is nothing to laugh at," he said. And suddenly he could not stop himself: he laughed. The door opened and my stepmother looked in while we were both shaking with laughter. My father laughed as if he were laughing for the first time for many years; his bounderish look, sly and bumptious and so delicious, came back to him. The door closed.

He stopped laughing.

"She might have been killed," he said, severely again.

"No, no, no," I cried, and tears came to my eyes.

He put his arm round me.

My mother was a cat, they said, a wicked woman, leaving us like that. I longed for my mother.

Three days later, I went camping. I apologized to my stepmother and she forgave me. I never saw her again.

SWEET TOWN

Toni Cade Bambara

UNITED STATES

It is hard to believe that there was only one spring and one summer apiece that year, my fifteenth year. It is hard to believe that I so quickly squandered my youth in the sweet town playground of the sunny city, that wild monkeybardom of my fourth-grade youthhood. However, it was so.

"Dear Mother"—I wrote one day on her bathroom mirror with a candle sliver—"please forgive my absence and my decay and overlook the freckled dignity and pockmarked integrity plaguing me this season."

I used to come on even wilder sometimes and write her mad cryptic notes on the kitchen sink with charred matches. Anything for a bit, we so seldom saw each other. I even sometimes wrote her a note on paper. And then one day, having romped my soul through the spectrum of sunny colors, I dashed up to her apartment to escape the heat and found a letter from her which eternally elated my heart to the point of bursture and generally endeared her to me forever. Written on the kitchen table in cake frosting was the message, "My dear, mad, perverse young girl, kindly take care and paint the fire escape in your leisure . . ." All the *i*'s were dotted with marmalade, the *t*'s were crossed with orange rind. Here was a sight to carry with one forever in the back of the screaming eyeballs somewhere. I howled for at least five minutes out of sheer madity and vowed to love her completely. Leisure. As if bare-armed spring ever let up from its invitation to perpetuate the race. And as if we ever owned a fire escape. "Zweep," I yelled, not giving a damn for intelligibility and decided that if ever I was to run away from home, I'd take her with me. And with that in mind, and with Penelope splintering through the landscape and the pores secreting animal champagne, I bent my youth to the season's tempo and proceeded to lose my mind.

There is a certain glandular disturbance all beautiful, wizardy, great people have second sight to, that trumpets through the clothes, sets the nerves up for the kill, and torments the senses to orange explosure. It has something to do with the cosmic interrelationship between the cellular attunement of certain designated organs and the firmental correlation with the axis shifts of the globe. My mother calls it sex and my brother says it's groin-fever time. But then, they were always ones for brevity. Anyway, that's the way it was. And in this spring race, the glands always win and the muses and the brain core must step aside to ride in the trunk with the spare tire. It was during this sweet and drugged madness time that I met B. J., wearing his handsomeness like an article of clothing, for an effect, and wearing his friend Eddie like a necessary pimple of adolescence. It was on the beach that we met, me looking great in a pair of cut-off dungarees and them with beards. Never mind the snows of yesteryear, I told myself, I'll take the sand and sun blizzard any day.

"Listen, Kit," said B. J. to me one night after we had experienced such we-encounters with the phenomenal world at large as a two-strawed mocha, duo-jaywalking summons, twosome whistling scenes, and other such like we-experiences, "the thing for us to do is hitch to the Coast and get into films."

"Righto," said Ed. "And soon."

"Sure thing, honeychile," I said, and jumped over an unknown garbage can. "We were made for celluloid—beautifully chiseled are we, not to mention well-buffed." I ran up and down somebody's stoop, whistling "Columbia the Gem of the Ocean" through my nose. And Eddie made siren sounds and walked a fence. B. J. grasped a parking-sign pole and extended himself parallel to the ground. I applauded, not only the gymnastics but also the offer. We liked to make bold directionless overtures to action like those crazy teenagers you're always running into on the printed page or in MGM movies.

"We could buy a sleeping bag," said B. J., and challenged a store cat to duel.

"We could buy a sleeping bag," echoed Eddie, who never had any real contribution to make in the say of statements.

"Three in a bag," I said while B. J. grasped me by the belt and we went flying down a side street. "Hrumph," I coughed, and perched on a fire hydrant. "Only one bag?"

"Of course," said B. J.

"Of course," said Ed. "And hrumph."

We came on like this the whole summer, even crazier. All of our friends abandoned us, they couldn't keep the pace. My mother threatened me with disinheritance. And my old roommate from camp actually turned the hose on me one afternoon in a fit of Florence Nightingale therapy. But hand in hand, me and Pan, and Eddie too, whizzed through the cement kaleidoscope making our own crazy patterns, singing our own song. And then one night a crazy thing happened. I dreamt that B. J. was running down the street howling, tearing his hair out and making love to the garbage cans on the boulevard. I was there laughing my head off and Eddie was spinning a beer bottle with a faceless person I didn't even know. I woke up and screamed for no reason I know of and my roommate, who was living with

us, threw a saltine cracker at me in way of saying something
about silence, peace, consideration, and sleepdom. And then
on top of that another crazy thing happened. Pebbles were flying into my opened window. The whole thing struck me funny.
It wasn't a casement window and there was no garden underneath. I naturally laughed my head off and my roommate got
really angry and cursed me out viciously. I explained to her
that pebbles were coming in, but she wasn't one for imagination and turned over into sleepdom. I went to the window to
see who I was going to share my balcony scene with, and there
below, standing on the milkbox, was B. J. I climbed out and
joined him on the stoop.

"What's up?" I asked, ready to take the world by storm in
my mixed-match baby-doll pajamas. B. J. motioned me into the
foyer and I could see by the distraught mask that he was wearing that serious discussion was afoot.

"Listen, Kit," he began, looking both ways with unnecessary caution. "We're leaving, tonight, now. Me and Eddie. He
stole some money from his grandmother, so we're cutting out."

"Where're ya going?" I asked. He shrugged. And just then I
saw Eddie dash across the stoop and into the shadows. B. J.
shrugged and he made some kind of desperate sound with his
voice like a stifled cry. "It's been real great. The summer and
you . . . but . . ."

"Look here," I said with anger. "I don't know why the hell
you want to hang around with that nothing." I was really angry
but sorry too. It wasn't at all what I wanted to say. I would have
liked to have said, "Apollo, we are the only beautiful people in
the world. And because our genes are so great, our kid can't
help but burst through the human skin into cosmic signifi-
cance." I wanted to say, "You will bear in mind that I am great,
brilliant, talented, good-looking, and am going to college at fifteen. I have the most interesting complexes ever, and despite

Freud and Darwin I have made a healthy adjustment as an earthworm." But I didn't tell him this. Instead, I revealed that petty, small, mean side of me by saying "Eddie is a shithead."

B. J. scratched his head, swung his foot in an arc, groaned, and took off. "Maybe next summer . . ." he started to say but his voice cracked and he and Eddie went dashing down the night street, arm in arm. I stood there with my thighs bare and my soul shook. Maybe we will meet next summer, I told the mailboxes. Or maybe I'll quit school and bum around the country. And in every town I'll ask for them as the hotel keeper feeds the dusty, weary traveler that I'll be. "Have you seen two guys, one great, the other acned? If you see 'em, tell 'em Kit's looking for them." And I'd bandage up my cactus-torn feet and sling the knapsack into place and be off. And in the next town, having endured dust storms, tornadoes, earthquakes, and coyotes, I'll stop at the saloon and inquire. "Yeh, they travel together," I'd say in a voice somewhere between W. C. Fields and Gladys Cooper. "Great buddies. Inseparable. Tell 'em for me that Kit's still a great kid."

And legends'll pop up about me and my quest. Great long twelve-bar blues ballads with eighty-nine stanzas. And a strolling minstrel will happen into the feedstore where B. J.'ll be and hear and shove the farmer's daughter off his lap and mount up to find me. Or maybe we won't meet ever, or we will but I won't recognize him cause he'll be an enchanted frog or a bald-headed fat man and I'll be God knows what. No matter. Days other than the here and now, I told myself, will be dry and sane and sticky with the rotten apricots oozing slowly in the sweet time of my betrayed youth.

BIG FISH, LITTLE FISH

Italo Calvino

ITALY

Zeffirino's father never wore a proper bathing suit. He would put on rolled-up shorts and an undershirt, a white duck cap on his head; and he never moved from the rocky shore. His passion was limpets, the flat mollusks that cling to the rocks until their terribly hard shell virtually becomes part of the rock itself. Zeffirino's father used a knife to prize them loose. Every Sunday, with his bespectacled stare, he passed in review, one by one, all the rocks along the point. He kept on until his little basket was full of limpets; some he ate as he collected them, sucking the moist, hard flesh as if from a spoon; the others he put in a basket. Every now and then he raised his eyes to glance, somewhat bewildered, over the smooth sea, and call, "Zeffirino! Where are you?"

Zeffirino spent whole afternoons in the water. The two of them went out to the point; his father would leave him there, then go off at once after his shellfish. Stubborn and motionless as they were, the limpets held no attraction for Zeffirino; it was the crabs, first and foremost, that interested him, then polyps, medusas, and so on, through all the varieties of fish. In the summer his pursuit became more difficult and ingenious; and by now there wasn't a boy his age who could handle a spear gun as well as he could. In the water, those stocky kids, all breath and muscle, are the best; and that's how Zeffirino was growing up. Seen on the shore, holding his father's hand, he looked like one of those kids with cropped hair and gaping mouth who have to be slapped to make them move. In the water, however, he outstripped them all; and, even better, underwater.

That day Zeffirino had managed to assemble a complete kit for underwater fishing. He had had the mask since the previous year, a present from his grandmother; a cousin whose feet were small had lent him her fins; he took the spear gun from his uncle's house without saying anything, but told his father it had been lent him, too. Actually, he was a careful boy, who knew how to use and take care of things, and he could be trusted if he borrowed something.

The sea was beautiful and clear. Zeffirino answered "Yes, Papà" to all the usual warnings, and went into the water. With the glass mask and the snorkel for breathing, with his legs ending like fish, and with that object in his hand—half gun and half spear and a little bit like a pitchfork, too—he no longer resembled a human being. Instead, once in the sea, though he darted off half submerged, you immediately recognized him as himself: from the kick he gave with the fins, from the way the gun jutted out beneath his arm, from his determination as he proceeded, his head at the surface of the water.

The sea bed was pebbles at first, then rocks, some of them bare and eroded, others bearded with thick, dark seaweed. From every cranny of the rocks, or among the tremulous beards swaying in the current, a big fish might suddenly appear; from behind the glass of the mask Zeffirino cast his eyes around, eagerly, intently.

A sea bed seems beautiful the first time, when you discover it; but, as with all things, the really beautiful part comes later, when you learn everything, stroke by stroke. You feel as if you were drinking them in, the aquatic trails: you go on and on and never want to stop. The glass of the mask is an enormous, single eye for swallowing colors and shadows. Now the dark ended, and he was beyond that sea of rock. On the sand of the bottom, fine wrinkles could be discerned, traced by the movement of the sea. The sun's rays penetrated all the way down, winking and flashing, and there was the glint of schools of hook-chasers, those tiny fish that swim in a very straight line, then suddenly, all of them together, make a sharp right turn.

A little puff of sand rose and it was the switching tail of a sea bream, there on the bottom. It wasn't even aware that the spear gun was aimed directly at it. Zeffirino was now swimming totally underwater; and the bream, after a few absent flicks of its striped sides, suddenly sped off at mid-depth. Among rocks bristling with sea urchins, the fish and the fisherman swam to an inlet with porous, almost bare rock. He can't get away from me here, Zeffirino thought; and at that moment the bream vanished. From nooks and hollows a stream of little air bubbles rose, then promptly ceased, to resume somewhere else. The sea anemones glowed, expectant. The bream peered from one lair, vanished into another, and promptly popped out from a distant gap. It skirted a spur of rock, headed downward. Zeffirino saw a patch of luminous green toward the bottom; the fish became lost in that light, and he dived after it.

He passed through a low arch at the foot of the cliff, and found the deep water and the sky above him again. Shadows of pale stone surrounded the bed, and out toward the open sea they descended, a half-submerged breakwater. With a twist of his hips and a thrust of the fins, Zeffirino surfaced to breathe. The snorkel surfaced, he blew out some drops that had infiltrated the mask; but the boy kept his head in the water. He had found the bream again: two bream, in fact! He was already taking aim when he saw a whole squadron of them proceeding calmly to the left, while another school glistened on the right. This was a place rich in fish, like an enclosed pond; and wherever Zeffirino looked he saw a flicker of sharp fins, the glint of scales; his joy and wonder were so great, he forgot to shoot even once.

The thing was not to be in a hurry, to study the best shots, and not to sow panic on all sides. Keeping his head down, Zeffirino moved toward the nearest rock; along its face, in the water, he saw a white hand swaying. The sea was motionless; on the taut and polished surface, concentric circles spread out, as if raindrops were falling. The boy raised his head and looked. Lying prone on the edge of the rock shelf, a fat woman in a bathing suit was taking the sun. And she was crying. Her tears ran down her cheeks one after another and dropped into the sea.

Zeffirino pushed his mask up on his forehead and said, "Excuse me."

The fat woman said, "Make yourself at home, kid." And she went on crying. "Fish as much as you like."

"This place is full of fish," he explained. "Did you see how many there are?"

The fat woman kept her head raised, her eyes staring straight ahead, filled with tears. "I didn't see anything. How could I? I can't stop crying."

As long as it was a matter of sea and fish, Zeffirino was the smartest; but in the presence of people, he resumed his gaping, stammering air. "I'm sorry, signora. . . ." He would have liked to get back to his bream, but a fat, crying woman was such an unusual sight that he stayed there, spellbound, gaping at her in spite of himself.

"I'm not a signora, kid," the fat woman said with her

noble, somewhat nasal voice. "Call me 'signorina.' Signorina De Magistris. And what's your name?"

"Zeffirino."

"Well, fine, Zeffirino. How's the fishing—or the shooting? VVhat do you call it?"

"I don't know what they call it. So far I haven't caught anything. But this is a good place."

"Be careful with that gun, though. I don't mean for my sake, poor me. I mean for you. Take care you don't hurt yourself."

Zeffirino assured her she needn't worry. He sat down on the rock beside her and watched her cry for a while. There were moments when it looked as if she might stop, and she sniffed with her reddened nose, raising and shaking her head. But meanwhile, at the corners of her eyes and under her lids, a bubble of tears seemed to swell until her eyes promptly brimmed over.

Zeffirino didn't know quite what to think. Seeing a lady cry was a thing that made your heart ache. But how could anyone be sad in this enclosure of sea crammed with every variety of fish to fill the heart with desire and joy? And how could you dive into that greenness and pursue fish when there was a grown-up person nearby dissolved in tears? At the same moment, in the same place, two yearnings existed, opposed and unreconcilable, but Zeffirino could neither conceive of them both together, nor surrender to the one or to the other.

"Signorina?" he asked.

"Yes?"

"Why are you crying?"

"Because I'm unlucky in love."

"Ah!"

"You can't understand; you're still a kid."

"You want to try swimming with my mask?"

"Thank you very much. Is it nice?"

"It's the nicest thing in the world."

Signorina De Magistris got up and fastened the straps of her suit at the back. Zeffirino gave her the mask and carefully explained how to put it on. She shook her head a little, half joking and half embarrassed, with the mask over her face; but behind it you could see her eyes, which didn't stop crying for a moment. She stepped into the water awkwardly, like a seal, and began paddling, holding her face down.

The gun under his arm, Zeffirino also went in swimming.

"When you see a fish, tell me," he shouted to the signorina. In the water he didn't fool around; and the privilege of coming out fishing with him was one he granted rarely.

But the signorina raised her head and shook it. The glass had clouded over and her features were no longer visible. She took off the mask. "I can't see anything," she said. "My tears make the glass cloud over. I can't. I'm sorry." And she stood there crying in the water.

"This is bad," Zeffirino said. He hadn't brought along a half of a potato, which you can rub on the glass to clear it again; but he did the best he could with some spit, then put the mask on himself. "Watch me," he said to the fat lady. And they proceeded together through that sea, he all fins, his head down, she swimming on her side, one arm extended and the other bent, her head bitterly erect and inconsolable.

She was a poor swimmer, Signorina De Magistris, always on her side, making clumsy, stabbing strokes. And beneath her, for yards, the fish raced through the sea, starfish and squid navigated, anemones yawned. Now Zeffirino's gaze saw landscapes approaching that would dazzle anyone. The water was deep, and the sandy bed was dotted with little stones among which skeins of seaweed swayed in the barely perceptible motion of the sea—though, observed from above, the rocks themselves seem to sway on the uniform expanse of sand, in the midst of the still water dense with seaweed.

All of a sudden, the signorina saw him disappear, head down, his behind surfacing for a moment, then the fins; and then his pale shadow was underwater, dropping toward the bottom. It was the moment when the bass realized the danger: the trident spear, already fired, caught him obliquely, and its central prong drove through his tail and transfixed him. The bass raised its prickly fins and lunged, slapping the water; the other prongs of the spear hadn't hooked him, and he still hoped to escape by sacrificing his tail. But all he achieved was to catch a fin on one of the other prongs; and so he was a goner. Zeffirino was already winding in the line, and the boy's pink and happy shadow fell above the fish.

The spear rose from the water with the bass impaled on it, then the boy's arm, then the masked head, with a gurgle of water from the snorkel. And Zeffirino bared his face: "Isn't he a beauty? Eh, signorina?" The bass was big, silvery and black. But the woman continued crying.

Zeffirino climbed up on the tip of a rock. With some effort, Signorina De Magistris followed him. To keep the fish fresh, the boy picked a little natural basin, full of water. They crouched down beside it. Zeffirino gazed at the iridescent colors of the bass, stroked its scales, and invited the signorina to do the same.

"You see how beautiful he is? You see how prickly?" When it looked as if a shaft of interest was piercing the fat lady's gloom, he said, "I'll just go off for a moment to see if I can catch another." And, fully equipped, he dived in.

The woman stayed behind with the fish. And she discovered that never had a fish been more unhappy. Now she ran her fingers over its ring-shaped mouth, along its fins, its tail. She saw a thousand tiny holes in its handsome silver body: sea lice, minuscule parasites of fish, had long since taken possession of the bass and were gnawing their way into its flesh.

Unaware of this, Zeffirino was already emerging again with a gilded umbra on the spear; and he held it out to Signorina De Magistris. The two had already divided their tasks: the woman took the fish off the prongs and put it in the pool, and Zeffirino stuck his head back into the water to go catch something else. But each time he first looked to see if the signorina had stopped crying: if the sight of a bass or an umbra wouldn't make her stop, what could possibly console her?

Gilded streaks marked the sides of the umbra. Two fins, parallel, ran down its back. And in the space between these fins, the signorina saw a deep, narrow wound, antedating those of the spear gun. A gull's beak must have pecked the fish's back with such force it was hard to figure out why it hadn't killed the fish. She wondered how long the umbra had been swimming around bearing that pain.

Faster than Zeffirino's spear, down toward a school of tiny, hesitant spicara, the sea bream plunged. He barely had time to gulp down one of the little fish before the spear stuck in his throat. Zeffirino had never fired such a good shot.

"A champion fish!" he cried, taking off his mask. "I was following the little ones! He swallowed one, and then I . . ." And he described the scene, stammering with emotion. It was impossible to catch a bigger, more beautiful fish; Zeffirino would have liked the signorina finally to share his contentment. She looked at the fat, silvery body, the throat that had just swallowed the little greenish fish, only to be ripped by the teeth of the spear: such was life throughout the sea.

In addition, Zeffirino caught a little gray fish and a red fish, a yellow-striped bream, a plump gilthead, and a flat bogue; even a mustached, spiky gurnard. But in all of them, besides the wounds of the spear, Signorina De Magistris discovered the bites of the lice that had gnawed them, or the stain of some unknown affliction, or a hook stuck for ages in the throat. This inlet the boy had discovered, where all sorts of fish gathered, was perhaps a refuge for animals sentenced to a long agony, a marine lazaretto, an arena of desperate duels.

Now Zeffirino was venturing along the rocks: octopus! He had come upon a colony squatting at the foot of a boulder. On the spear one big purplish octopus now emerged, a liquid like watered ink dripping from its wounds; and a strange uneasiness overcame Signorina De Magistris. To keep the octopus they found a more secluded basin, and Zeffirino wanted never to leave it, to stay and admire the gray-pink skin that slowly changed hues. It was late, too, and the boy was beginning to get a bit of gooseflesh, his swim had lasted so long. But Zeffirino was hardly one to renounce a whole family of octopus, now discovered.

The signorina observed the octopus, its slimy flesh, the mouths of the suckers, the reddish and almost liquid eye. Alone among the whole catch, the polyp seemed to be without blemish or torment. The tentacles of an almost human pink, so limp and sinuous and full of secret armpits, prompted thoughts of health and life, and some lazy contractions caused them to twist still, with a slight opening of the suckers. In mid-air, the hand of Signorina De Magistris sketched a caress over the coils of the octopus; her fingers moved to imitate its contraction, closer and closer, and finally touched the coils lightly.

Evening was falling; a wave began to slap the sea. The tentacles vibrated in the air like whips, and suddenly, with all its strength, the octopus was clinging to the arm of Signorina De Magistris. Standing on the rock, as if fleeing from her own imprisoned arm, she let out a cry that sounded like: It's the octopus! The octopus is torturing me!

Zeffirino, who at that very moment had managed to flush

a squid, stuck his head out of the water and saw the fat woman with the octopus, which stretched out one tentacle from her arm to catch her by the throat. He also heard the end of the scream: it was a high, constant scream, but—so it seemed to the boy—without tears.

A man armed with a knife rushed up and started aiming blows at the octopus's eye. He decapitated it almost with one stroke. This was Zeffirino's father, who had filled his basket with limpets and was searching along the rocks for his son. Hearing the cry, narrowing his bespectacled gaze, he had seen the woman and run to help her, with the blade he used for his limpets. The tentacles immediately relaxed; Signorina De Magistris fainted.

When she came to, she found the octopus cut into pieces, and Zeffirino and his father made her a present of it, so she could fry it. It was evening, and Zeffirino put on his shirt. His father, with precise gestures, explained to her the secret of a good octopus fry. Zeffirino looked at her and several times thought she was about to start up again; but no, not a single tear came from her.

—TRANSLATED BY WILLIAM WEAVER

INEM

Pramoedya Ananta Toer

INDONESIA

Inem was one of the girls I knew. She was eight years old—two years older than me. She was no different from the others. And if there was a difference, it was that she was one of the prettier little girls in our neighborhood. People liked to look at her. She was polite, unspoiled, deft, and hard-working—qualities which quickly spread her fame even into other neighborhoods as a girl who would make a good daughter-in-law.

And once when she was heating water in the kitchen, she said to me, "Gus* Muk, I'm going to be married."

"You're fooling!" I said.

"No, the proposal came a week ago. Mama and Papa and all the relatives have accepted the proposal."

"What fun to be a bride!" I exclaimed happily.

"Yes, it'll be fun, I know it will! They'll buy me all sorts of nice clothes. I'll be dressed up in a bride's outfit, with flowers in my hair, and they'll make me up with powder and mascara. Oh, I'll like that!"

---

*Gus: A title of respect that Inem, as a servant, uses toward the son of the family for whom she works.

And it was true. One afternoon her mother called on mine. At that time Inem was living with us as a servant. Her daily tasks were to help with the cooking and to watch over me and my younger brothers and sisters as we played.

Inem's mother made a living by doing batik work. That was what the women in our neighborhood did when they were not working in the rice fields. Some put batik designs on sarongs, while others worked on head cloths. The poorer ones preferred to do head cloths; since it did not take so long to finish a head cloth, they received payment for it sooner. And Inem's mother supported her family by putting batik designs on head cloths. She got the cloth and the wax from her employer, the Idjo Store. For every two head cloths that she finished, she was paid one and a half cents. On the average, a woman could do eight to eleven head cloths a day.

Inem's father kept gamecocks. All he did, day after day, was to wager his bird in cockfights. If he lost, the victor would take his cock. And in addition he would have to pay two and a half rupiahs, or at the very least seventy-five cents. When he was not gambling on cockfights, he would play cards with his neighbors for a cent a hand.

Sometimes Inem's father would be away from home for a month or half a month, wandering around on foot. His return would signify that he was bringing home some money.

Mother once told me that Inem's father's main occupation had been robbing people in the teak forest between our town, Blora, and the coastal town of Rembang. I was then in the first grade, and heard many stories of robbers, bandits, thieves, and murderers. As a result of those stories and what Mother told me, I came to be terrified of Inem's father.

Everybody knew that Inem's father was a criminal, but no one could prove it and no one dared complain to the police. Consequently he was never arrested by the police. Furthermore, almost all of Inem's mother's relatives were policemen. There was even one with the rank of agent first class. Inem's father himself had once been a policeman but had been discharged for taking bribes.

Mother also told me that in the old days Inem's father had been an important criminal. As a way of countering an outbreak of crime that was getting out of hand, the Netherlands Indies government had appointed him a policeman, so that he could round up his former associates. He never robbed any more after that, but in our area he continued to be a focus of suspicion.

When Inem's mother called on my mother, Inem was heating water in the kitchen. I tagged along after Inem's mother. The visitor, Mother, and I saw on a low, red couch.

"Ma'am," said Inem's mother, "I've come to ask for Inem to come back home."

"Why do you want Inem back? Isn't it better for her to be here? You don't have any of her expenses, and here she can learn how to cook."

"Yes, ma'am, but I plan for her to get married after the coming harvest."

"What?" exclaimed Mother, startled. "She's going to be married?"

"Yes, ma'am. She's old enough to be married now—she's eight years old," said Inem's mother.

At this my mother laughed. And her visitor was surprised to see Mother laugh.

"Why, a girl of eight is still a child!" said Mother.

"We're not upper-class people, ma'am. I think she's already a year too old. You know Asih? She married her daughter when she was two years younger than mine."

Mother tried to dissuade the woman. But Inem's mother had another argument. Finally the visitor spoke again: "I feel lucky that someone wants her. If we let a proposal go by this time, maybe there will never be another one. And how humiliating it would be to have a daughter turn into an old maid! And it just might be that if she gets married she'll be able to help out with the household expenses."

Mother did not reply. Then she looked at me and said; "Go get the betel* set and the spittoon."

So I went to fetch the box of betel-chewing ingredients and the brass spittoon.

"And what does your husband say?"

"Oh, he agrees. What's more, Markaban is the son of a well-to-do man—his only child. Markaban has already begun to help his father trade cattle in Rembang, Tjepu, Medang, Pati, Ngawen, and also here in Blora," said Inem's mother.

This information seemed to cheer Mother up, although I could not understand why. Then she called Inem, who was at work in the kitchen. Inem came in. And Mother asked, "Inem, do you want to get married?"

Inem bowed her head. She was very respectful toward Mother. I never once heard her oppose her. Indeed, it is rare to find people who are powerless opposing anything that others say to them.

I saw then that Inem was beaming. She often looked like that; give her something that pleased her even a little and she would beam. But she was not accustomed to saying "thank you." In the society of the simple people of our neighborhood, the words "thank you" were still unfamiliar. It was only through the glow radiating from their faces that gratitude found expression.

"Yes, ma'am," said Inem so softly as to be almost inaudible.

Then Inem's mother and mine chewed some betel. Mother herself did not like to chew betel all the time. She did it only

---

*betel: A plant whose leaves are chewed by many Asians.

when she had a woman visitor. Every few moments she would spit into the brass spittoon.

When Inem had gone back to the kitchen Mother said, "It's not right to make children marry."

These words surprised Inem's mother. But she did not say anything nor did her eyes show any interest.

"I was eighteen when I got married," said Mother.

Inem's mother's surprise vanished. She was no longer surprised now, but she still did not say anything.

"It's not right to make children marry," repeated Mother.

And Inem's mother was surprised again.

"Their children will be stunted."

Inem's mother's surprise vanished once more.

"Yes, ma'am." Then she said placidly, "My mother was also eight when she got married."

Mother paid no attention and continued, "Not only will they be stunted, but their health will be affected too."

"Yes, ma'am, but ours is a long-lived family. My mother is still alive, though she's over fifty-nine. And my grandmother is still alive too. I think she must be seventy-four. She's still vigorous and strong enough to pound corn in the mortar."

Still ignoring her, Mother went on, "Especially if the husband is also a child."

"Yes, ma'am, but Markaban is seventeen."

"Seventeen! My husband was thirty when he married me."

Inem's mother was silent. She never stopped shifting the wad of tobacco leaves that was stuck between her lips. One moment she would move the tobacco to the right, a moment later to the left, and the next moment she would roll it up and scrub her coal-black teeth with it.

Now Mother had no more arguments with which to oppose her visitor's intention. She said, "Well, if you've made up your mind to marry Inem off, I only hope that she gets a good husband who can take care of her. And I hope she gets someone who is compatible."

Inem's mother left, still shifting the tobacco about in her mouth.

"I hope nothing bad happens to that child."

"Why would anything bad happen to her?" I asked.

"Never mind, Muk, it's nothing." Then Mother changed the subject. "If the situation of their family improves, we won't lose any more of our chickens."

"Is somebody stealing our chickens, Mama?" I asked.

"No, Muk, never mind," Mother said slowly. "Such a little child! Only eight years old. What a pity it is. But they need money. And the only way to get it is to marry off their daughter."

Then Mother went to the garden behind the house to get some string beans for supper.

Fifteen days after this visit, Inem's mother came again to fetch her daughter. She seemed greatly pleased that Inem made no objection to being taken away. And when Inem was about to leave our house, never to be a member of our family again, she spoke to me in the kitchen doorway, "Well, good bye, Gus Muk. I'm going home, Gus Muk," she said very softly.

She always spoke softly. Speaking softly was one of the customary ways of showing politeness in our small-town society. She went off as joyfully as a child who expects to be given a new blouse.

From that moment, Inem no longer lived in our house. I felt very deeply the loss of my constant companion. From that moment also, it was no longer Inem who took me to the bathing cubicle at night to wash my feet before going to bed, but my adoptive older sister.

Sometime I felt an intense longing to see Inem. Not infrequently, when I had got into bed, I would recall the moment when her mother drew her by the hand and the two of them left our house. Inem's house was in back of ours, separated only by a wooden fence.

She had been gone a month. I often went to her house to play with her, and Mother always got angry when she found out that I had been there. She would always say, "What can you learn at Inem's house that's of any use?"

And I would never reply. Mother always had a good reason for scolding me. Everything she said built a thick wall that was impenetrable to excuses. Therefore my best course was to be silent. And as the clinching argument in her lecture, she was almost certain to repeat the sentences that she uttered so often: "What's the point to your playing with her? Aren't there lots of other children you can ask to play with you? What's more, she's a woman who's going to be married soon."

But I kept on sneaking over to her house anyway. It is surprising sometimes how a prohibition seems to exist solely in order to be violated. And when I disobeyed I felt that what I did was pleasurable. For children such as I at that time—oh, how many prohibitions and restrictions were heaped on our heads! Yes, it was as though the whole world was watching us, bent on forbidding whatever we did and whatever we wanted. Inevitably we children felt that this world was really intended only for adults.

Then the day of the wedding arrived.

For five days before the ceremony, Inem's family was busy in the kitchen, cooking food and preparing various delicacies. This made me visit her house all the more frequently.

The day before the wedding, Inem was dressed in all her finery. Mother sent me there with five kilos of rice and twenty-five cents as a neighborly contribution. And that afternoon we children crowded around and stared at her in admiration. The hair over her forehead and temples and her eyebrows had been carefully trimmed with a razor and thickened with mascara. Her little bun of hair had been built up with a switch and adorned with the paper flowers with springs for stalks that we call *sunduk mentul.* Her clothes were made of satin. Her sarong was an expensive one made in Solo. These things had all been rented from a Chinaman in the Chinese quarter near the town square. The gold rings and bracelets were all rented too.

The house was decorated with constructions of banyan leaves and young coconut fronds. On each wall there were crossed tricolor flags encircled by palm leaves. All the house pillars were similarly decorated with tricolor bunting.

Mother herself went and helped with the preparations. But not for long. Mother rarely did this sort of thing except for her closest neighbors. She stayed less than an hour. And it was then too that the things sent by Inem's husband-to-be arrived: a load of cakes and candies, a male goat, a quantity of rice, a packet of salt, a sack of husked coconuts, and half a sack of granulated sugar.

It was just after the harvest. Rice was cheap. And when rice was cheap all other footstuffs were cheap too. That was why the period after the harvest was a favorite time for celebrations. And for that reason Inem's family had found it impossible to contract for a puppet performance. The puppet masters had already been engaged by other families in various neighborhoods. The puppet theater was the most popular form of entertainment in our area. In our town there were three types of puppet performance: the *wajan purwa* or shadow play, which recounted stories from the *Mahabharata* and the *Ramayana,* as well as other stories similar in theme; the *wajang krutjil,* in which wooden puppets in human shape acted out stories of Arabia, Persia, India, and China, as well as tales of Madjapahit times; and the *wajang golek*, which employed wooden dolls. But this last was not very popular.

Because there were no puppet masters available, Inem's family engaged a troupe of dancing girls. At first this created a dispute. Inem's relatives on her mother's side were religious scholars and teachers. But Inem's father would not back down. The dance troupe came, with its *gamelan* orchestra, and put on a *tajuban*.

Usually, in our area, a *tajuban* was attended by the men who wanted to dance with the girls and by little children who only wanted to watch—little children whose knowledge of sexual matters did not go beyond kissing. The grown boys did not like to watch; it embarrassed them. This was even more the case with the women—none of them attended at all. And a *tajuban* in our area—in order to inflame sexual passions—was always accompanied by alcoholic beverages: arrack, beer, whisky, or gin.

The *tajuban* lasted for two days and nights. We children took great delight in the spectacle of men and women dancing and kissing one another and every now and then clinking their glasses and drinking liquor as they danced and shouted, "*Huse!*"

And though Mother forbade me to watch, I went anyway on the sly.

"Why do you insist on going where those wicked people are? Look at your religious teacher: he doesn't go to watch, even though he is Inem's father's brother-in-law. You must have noticed that yourself."

Our religious teacher also had a house in back of ours, to the right of Inem's house. Subsequently the teacher's failure to attend became a topic that was sure to enliven a conversation. From it there arose two remarks that itched on the tip of everyone's tongue: that the teacher was certainly a pious man, and that Inem's father was undoubtedly a reprobate.

Mother reinforced her scolding with words that I did not understand at the time: "Do you know something? They are people who have no respect for women," she said in a piercing voice.

And when the bridegroom came to be formally presented to the bride, Inem, who had been sitting on the nuptial seat, was led forth. The bridegroom had reached the veranda. Inem squatted and made obeisance to her future husband, and then washed his feet with flower water from a brass pot. Then the couple were tied together and conducted side by side to the nuptial seat. At that time the onlookers could be heard saying, "One child becomes two. One child becomes two. One child becomes two."

And the women who were watching beamed as though they were to be the recipients of the happiness to come.

At that very moment I noticed that Inem was crying so much that her make-up was spoiled, and tears were trickling down her face. At home I asked Mother, "Why was the bride crying, Mama?"

"When a bride cries, it's because she is thinking of her long-departed ancestors. Their spirits also attend the ceremony. And they are happy that their descendant has been safely married," replied Mother.

I never gave any thought to those words of hers. Later I found out why Inem had been crying. She had to urinate, but was afraid to tell anyone.

The celebration ended uneventfully. There were no more guests coming with contributions. The house resumed its everyday appearance, and by the time the moneylenders came to collect, Inem's father had left Blora. After the wedding, Inem's mother and Inem herself went on doing batik work— day and night. And if someone went to their house at three o'clock in the morning, he would be likely to find them still working. Puffs of smoke would be rising between them from the crucible in which the wax was melted. In addition to that, quarreling was often heard in that house.

And once, when I was sleeping with Mother in her bed, a loud scream awakened me: "I won't! I won't!"

It was still night then. The screams were repeated again and again, accompanied by the sound of blows and pounding on a door. I knew that the screams came from Inem's mouth. I recognized her voice.

"Mama, why is Inem screaming?" I asked.

"They're fighting. I hope nothing bad happens to that little girl," she said. But she gave no explanation.

"Why would anything bad happen to her, Mama?" I asked insistently.

Mother did not reply to my question. And then, when the screaming and shouting were over, we went back to sleep. Such screams were almost sure to be heard every night. Screams and screams. And every time I heard them, I would ask my mother about them. Mother would never give a satisfactory answer. Sometimes she merely sighed, "What a pity, such a little child!"

One day Inem came to our house. She went straight in to find my mother. Her face was pale, bloodless. Before saying anything, she set the tone of the occasion by crying—crying in a respectful way.

"Why are you crying, Inem? Have you been fighting again?" Mother asked.

"Ma'am," said Inem between her sobs, "I hope that you will be willing to take me back here as before."

"But you're married, aren't you, Inem?"

And Inem cried some more. Through her tears she said, "I can't stand it, ma'am."

"Why, Inem? Don't you like your husband?" asked Mother.

"Ma'am, please take pity on me. Every night all he wants to do is wrestle, ma'am."

"Can't you say to him, 'Please, dear, don't be like that'?"

"I'm afraid, ma'am. I'm afraid of him. He's so big. And when he wrestles he squeezes me so hard that I can't breathe. You'll take me back, won't you, ma'am?" she pleaded.

"If you didn't have a husband, Inem, of course I'd take you back. But you have a husband . . ."

And Inem cried again when she heard what Mother said. "Ma'am, I don't want to have a husband."

"You may not want to, but the fact is that you do, Inem. Maybe eventually your husband will change for the better, and the two of you will be able to live happily. You wanted to get married, didn't you?" said Mother.

"Yes, ma'am . . . but, but . . ."

"Inem, regardless of anything else, a woman must serve her husband faithfully. If you aren't a good wife to your husband, your ancestors will curse you," said Mother.

Inem began crying harder. And because of her crying she was unable to say anything.

"Now, Inem, promise me that you will always prepare your husband's meals. When you have an idle moment, you should pray to God to keep him safe. You must promise to wash his clothes, and you must massage him when he is tired from his work. You must rub his back vigorously when he catches cold."

Inem still made no reply. Only her tears continued to fall.

"Well, now, you go home, and from this moment on be a good wife to him. No matter whether he is good or bad, you must serve him faithfully, because after all he *is* your husband."

Inem, who was sitting on the floor, did not stir.

"Get up and go home to your husband. You . . . if you just

up and quit your husband the consequences will not be good for you, either now or in the future," Mother added.

"Yes, ma'am," Inem said submissively. Slowly she rose and walked home.

"How sad, she's so little," said Mother.

"Mama, does Daddy ever wrestle you?" I asked.

Mother looked searchingly into my eyes. Then her scrutiny relaxed. She smiled. "No," she said. "Your father is the best person in the whole world, Muk."

Then Mother went to the kitchen to get the hoe, and she worked in the garden with me.

A year passed imperceptibly. On a certain occasion Inem came again. In the course of a year she had grown much bigger. It was quite apparent that she was mature, although only nine years old. As usual, she went directly to where Mother was and sat on the floor with her head bowed. She said, "Ma'am, now I don't have a husband any more."

"What?"

"Now I don't have a husband any more."

"You're divorced?" asked Mother.

"Yes, ma'am."

"Why did you separate from him?"

She did not reply.

"Did you fail to be a good wife to him?"

"I think I was always a good wife to him, ma'am."

"Did you massage him when he came home tired from work?" asked Mother probingly.

"Yes, ma'am, I did everything you advised me to."

"Well, then, why did you separate?"

"Ma'am, he often beat me."

"Beat you? He beat a little child like you?"

"I did everything I could to be a good wife, ma'am. And

when he beat me and I was in pain—was that part of being a good wife, ma'am?" she asked, in genuine perplexity.

Mother was silent. Her eyes scrutinized Inem. "He beat you," Mother whispered then.

"Yes, ma'am—he beat me just the way Mama and Papa do."

"Maybe you failed in some way after all in your duty to him. A husband would never have the heart to beat a wife who was really and truly a good wife to him."

Inem did not reply. She changed the subject: "Would you be willing to take me back, ma'am?"

There was no hesitation in Mother's reply. She said firmly, "Inem, you're a divorced woman now. There are lots of grown boys here. It wouldn't look right to people, would it?"

"But they wouldn't beat me," said the divorcée.

"No. That isn't what I mean. It just doesn't look right for a divorced woman as young as you to be in a place where there are lots of men."

"Is it because there's something wrong with me, ma'am?"

"No, Inem, it's a question of propriety."

"Propriety, ma'am? It's for the sake of propriety that I can't stay here?"

"Yes, that's the way it is, Inem."

The divorcée did not say anything more. She remained sitting on the floor, and seemed to have no intention of leaving the place where she was sitting. Mother went up to her and patted her shoulder consolingly. "Now, Inem . . . the best thing is for you to help your parents earn a living. I really regret that I can't take you back here."

Two tears formed in the corners of the little woman's eyes. She got up. Listlessly she moved her feet, leaving our house to return to her parents' house. And from then on she was seldom seen outside her house.

And thereafter, the nine-year-old divorcée—since she was nothing but a burden to her family—could be beaten by anyone who wanted to: her mother, her brothers, her uncles, her neighbors, her aunts. Yet Inem never again came to our house.

Her screams of pain were often heard. When she moaned, I covered my ears with my hands. And Mother continued to uphold the respectability of her home.

—TRANSLATED BY RUFUS S HENDRON

THE CHILD WHO LOVED ROADS

Cora Sandel

NORWAY

Most of all she loved roads with the solitary track of a horse down the middle and with grass between the wheel ruts. Narrow old roads with lots of bends and nobody else around and here and there a piece of straw perhaps, fallen from a load of hay. The child turned springy and light as air on them, filled with happiness at breaking free, at existing. Behind each bend waited unknown possibilities, however many times you'd gone down the road. You could make them up yourself if nothing else.

Down the highway she walked, dragging her feet in dust and gravel. Dust and gravel were among the bad things in life. You got tired, hot, heavy, longed to be picked up and carried.

Then suddenly the narrow old road was there, and the child began to run, leaping high with happiness.

She hadn't been so tired after all, the grown-ups said. There's a lot grown-ups don't understand. You have to give up explaining anything to them and take them as they are, an inconvenience, for the most part. No one should grow up. No, children should stay children and rule the whole world. Everything would be more fun and a lot better then.

Early on the child learned that it was best to be alone on

the road. A good ways in front of the others anyway. Only then did you come to know the road as it really was, with its marks of wheels and horses hooves, its small, stubborn stones sticking up, its shifting lights and shadows. Only then did you come to know the fringes of the road, warm from sun and greenness, plump and furry with wild chervil and lady's mantle—altogether a strange and wonderful world unto itself, where you could wander free as you pleased, and everything was good, safe, and just the way you wanted it.

At least it was in the summer. In winter the road was something else entirely. In the twilight of a snow-gray day your legs could turn to lead, everything was so sad. You never seemed to get any further; there was always a long ways to go. The middle of the road was brown and ugly, like rice pudding with cinnamon on it, a dish that grew in her mouth and that she couldn't stand. People and trees stood out black and sorrowful against the white. You did have the sledding hill, the field with deep snow for rolling on, the courtyard for building forts and caves, the skis without real bindings. For small children shouldn't have real bindings, the grown-ups said; they could fall and break their legs. In the twilight everything was merely sad, and nothing about it could compare to the roads in summer.

To be let loose on them, without a jacket, without a hat, *bare*, that was life the way it should be. Only one thing compared to it, the hills at the big farm, where she was often a guest.

There were paths bordered with heather and crowberry leading up to views over the blue fjord and to a light, never-still breeze that tickled your scalp. White stone protruded from the heather and the path. At the bottom of the hill you found wild strawberries, higher up blueberries, not just a few either, and bilberries. On top lay the crowberries in patches like large carpets.

The child could pass hours lying on her stomach near a bush, stuffing herself, and at the same time thinking of all sorts of things. She possessed an active imagination, seldom longed for company and could sometimes fly into a rage if she got it.

"You're so contrary," said the grown-ups. "Can't you be nice and sweet like the others, just a little? You should be thankful anyone wants to be with you," they said.

"It won't be easy for you when you're older," they also said.

The child forgot it as soon as it was said. She ran off to the road or the paths and remembered nothing so unreasonable, so completely ridiculous.

One road went from the house on the big farm, went along the garden where huge old red currant bushes hung over the picket fence, casually offering their magnificence; the road went across the fields, bordered by thin young trees, made a leap over a hill and swung two times like an *S* before it wandered out in the world and became one with the boring highway.

The child's own road, newly taken possession of summer after summer. Here no one came running after you, here you could wander without company. Nothing could happen but the right things. If anyone came driving or riding it was uncles, aunts, or the farmboy. They saw you from a long distance away, they stopped; if they came by wagon you got a ride to the farm.

Here and on the hills were where the stories came into being, short ones and long ones. If they didn't look like they were living up to their promise, you just stopped and started a new one.

A place in life where freedom had no boundaries. Very different from what the grown-ups meant when they said, "in this life," or "in this world," and sighed. They also said, "in this difficult life." As if to make things as nasty as possible.

Being together with someone—that was sometimes fun and sometimes not at all. You couldn't explain why or why not; it was part of everything you imagined and that you'd never dream of talking to grown-ups about. On the contrary, you held tightly to it, like someone insisting on something wrong they've done. Maybe it was "wrong"; maybe it was one of those things that ought to be "rooted out of you." Or at best to laugh about a little, to whisper over your head.

"Constructive" it wasn't, in any case. They were always talking about the necessity of doing "constructive things."

It could be fun, when Alette came, Letta. She was a redhead, freckled, full of laughter, easy to get along with. At her house, at the neighboring farm, was a chest in the loft, full of old-fashioned clothes. Dresses in wonderful light colors, flounce after flounce on the wide tarlatan skirts, a name that was far prettier than, for example, blue cotton cambric. A man's suit, yellow knee breeches and a green coat with gold buttons, an unbelievable costume that didn't look like anything the uncles wore. A folding parasol, a whole collection of odd hats. To dress up in all that, strut around in it, stumble in the long skirts, mimic the grown-ups and make them laugh where they sat on the garden steps, was fun enough for a while. But it was nothing to base a life on.

For that you could only use the roads, the paths and the hills.

Grown-up, well, you probably had to turn into one. Everyone did; you couldn't avoid it.

But like some of them? Definitely not.

In the first place the child was going to run her whole life, never do anything so boring as walk slowly and deliberately. In the second and third place . . .

The grown-ups didn't have much that was worthwhile. It was true they got everything they wanted, could buy themselves things they wanted and go to bed when they felt like it, eat things at the table that children didn't get—all the best things, in short. They could command and scold, give canings and presents. But they got long skirts or trousers to wear and then they *walked. Just* walked. You had to wonder if it had something to do with what was called Confirmation, if there wasn't something about it that injured their legs. There probably was, since they hid them and walked. They *couldn't* run any longer. Even though—you saw them dance; you saw them play "Widower Seeks a Mate" and "Last Pair Out."

Maybe it was their minds something was wrong with?

Everything truly fun disappeared from their lives, and they let it happen. None of them rebelled. On the contrary, they grew conceited about their sad transformation. Was there anything so conceited as the big girls when they got long skirts and put up their hair!

They walked, they sat and embroidered, sat and wrote, sat and chatted, knitted, crocheted. Walked and sat, sat and walked. Stupid, they were so stupid!

Trailing skirts were dangerous. She'd have to watch out, when the time came. Run away, maybe.

At home, in the city street, were the mean boys.

Really big boys, the kind who were practically uncles, were often nice. They were the ones who organized the big circus in the empty lot, with trapeze artists, clowns, and tickets that the grown-ups bought in complete seriousness: parquet circle, first class, second class. A ringmaster in a tuxedo went around the circus ring and cracked his long whip at the horses doing tricks. A true circus, so to speak, except that the horses consisted of two boys under a blanket that sometimes sagged in the middle. But that was easy to overlook.

The big boys arranged competition races in the winter, saw to it that you got new skis and real bindings; they were pillars of support. One of them once got up and lambasted his sister, who had tattled on him. A bunch of lies, made up, shameful, that you just had to sit there and take, for you didn't get anywhere saying it wasn't true.

They were pillars all the same.

But there was a half-grown kind, a mean kind, that made such a racket. They ran back and forth with wooden bats in their hands and the balls shot between them like bullets. In the winter they threw hard snowballs, and if anyone had put up an especially fine fort anywhere, they came rushing down in a crowd and stormed it, left it destroyed. Sometimes they threatened you with a beating. For no reason, just to threaten. The child was deathly afraid of them, took any roundabout way she could to avoid them; she would rather be too late for dinner.

Sometimes she *had* to come through enemy lines to get home. With her heart in her throat, with her head bowed as if in a storm, she sneaked sideways along the walls of the houses. The taunts rained down.

One day a boy of that sort came after the child, grabbed her arm, squeezed it hard, and said, "You know what you are? Do you?"

No answer.

"You're just a girl. Go home where you belong."

Hard as a whip the words struck the child. Just a girl— *just*. From that moment she had a heavy burden to bear, one of the heaviest, the feeling of being something inferior, of being born that way, beyond help.

With such a burden on your back the world becomes a different place for you. Your sense of yourself begins to change.

But the roads remained an even bigger consolation than before. On them even "just a girl" felt easy, free, and secure.

The child was one of those who feels sorry. For skinny horses and horses who got the whip, for cats who looked homeless, for children who were smaller than she was and who didn't have mittens in winter, for people who just generally looked poor, and for drunken men.

Why she was so sorry for drunken men was never clear. They'd drunk hard liquor; they could have left it alone. They were their own worst enemies, the grown-ups explained; if things went so badly for them it was their own fault.

In the child's eyes they were nothing but helpless. They tumbled here and there; sometimes they fell down and remained lying there—the policeman came and dragged them off roughly. Sorry for them, she was sorry for them; they couldn't help it, they couldn't help it for anything, however they'd come to be that way. They were like little children who can't walk on their own and do things wrong because they don't know any better.

The child cried herself to sleep at times on account of the drunkards. And on account of the horses, cats, and poor people. Once you're like that, you don't have it easy. The cats she could have taken home if it hadn't been for the grown-ups. She wasn't allowed. As if one cat more or less mattered. You were power-less, in this as in everything.

On the summertime roads you forgot your troubles. If you met poorly clad people you usually knew who they were, where they lived, that they had nicer clothes at home that they saved for Sundays. The horses you met were rounded, comfortable, easygoing. They waved their long tails up over thick haunches and grazed by the roadside as soon as they got a chance. The cats rubbed against your legs, purring loudly. Farm cats who belonged somewhere and were just out for a walk.

You hardly ever met anyone, though, whether people or animals. That was what was wonderful; it became more and more wonderful as the child grew older. She had a steadily stronger desire to keep making up stories in her head. There was no place that they came so readily as along a two-wheeled track with grass in between. Or up on the hill where the breeze brushed your scalp.

Time passed. The child ran, long braid flapping, on the roads.

If she was overtaken by the grown-ups, she heard, "You're too old now to be running like that. Soon you'll be wearing long skirts, remember. A young lady *walks*, she holds herself nicely, thinks about how she places her feet. Then she can't rush away like you do."

The child ran even faster than before. To get out of earshot, out of range as much as possible. Her legs had grown long; they were an advantage when she took to her heels. The braid swung, the lengthened skirt swung. The child thought— one day I won't turn around when they call, I won't wait for anyone. That might be sooner than they suspect. The roads lead much farther than I realized; they lead out into the world, away from all of them.

When she stopped, she looked around with new eyes, seeing no longer just the roadsides, but the horizons. Behind them lay what she longed for, craved: freedom.

But one of the big boys, the kind who were practically uncles, suddenly popped out of nowhere. He was Letta's cousin, had passed his high school exams, was a university student.

You didn't see much of him. Letta said he was stupid and conceited, a self-important fellow who kept to his room or with the grown-ups. He himself was definitely not all that grown up, said Letta, who remembered him in short pants, remembered that he stole apples at someone's and got a caning for it at home. That wasn't so very long ago; she'd been ten years old, on a visit to his parents. Now she was thirteen, almost fourteen.

He had a strange effect on the child; he upset her from the

first moment in a way that was both painful and good. It was impossible to think of him when he was nearby and could turn up; you can't think when you're blushing in confusion. But out on the roads he crept into her thoughts to the extent that she couldn't get him out again; he took up residence there, inserted himself in the middle of an ongoing story, which had to be completely changed. There was no other recourse.

The story came to be about him. He became the main character, along with herself. In spite of the fact that she didn't really know how he looked; she never quite risked looking at him. And in spite of the fact that he wore long trousers, *walked*, and consequently belonged to the poor fool category.

It was inexplicable, and she felt it as slightly shameful, a defeat. The child grew fiery red with embarrassment if he so much as made an appearance. As the misfortune was written on her face, it was necessary to avoid Letta and her family, to keep to the roads as never before.

You could go into Letta's garden without being seen.

Letta followed, full of suggestions; she wanted them to get dressed up like summers before, to make fun of the cousin, who was sitting on the steps with the grown-ups—to mimic him.

"He doesn't interest me."

"You think he interests me? That's why we can tease him a little, can't we?"

"I'm not interested in teasing such a disgusting person," explained the child, marveling at her own words.

"Come anyway, though."

"No."

"Why not?"

"Because I don't want to, that's why."

But it was a terribly empty feeling, when Letta gave up and walked away. Just to talk about him was a new and remarkable experience, was something she yearned for, wanted and had to do.

The child was beginning to *walk* on the roads. Slowly even. She stood still for long moments at a time. For no reason, to fuss with the tie on her braid, to curl the end of the braid around her fingers, to scrape her toe in the gravel, to stare out into space. She sat down in the grass by the roadside, trailed her hand searchingly around between the lady's mantle and water avens, did it over and over.

Finally her hand had found something, a four-leaf clover. Thoughtfully the child walked on with it, holding it carefully between two fingers.

"Well, now, finally you're acting like a big girl," said one of the aunts, pleased. "Not a minute too soon. Good thing we don't have to nag you anymore. Good thing there's still a little hem to let out in your dress. Next week we'll get Joanna the seamstress."

Hardly was it said than the child set off at full speed, in defiance, in panic.

Without her having noticed it or understood it, she had allowed something to happen, something frightening, something detestable. Something that made *them* happy. But nothing should make them happy. For then they'd be getting you where they wanted you, a prisoner, some kind of invalid.

The child didn't hear the despairing sigh of a deeply worried grown-up. That would have made her relieved and calm. Instead she only felt torn by life's contradictions, bewildered and confused by them.

One day the cousin left; he was simply gone. Letta said, Who cares, he was conceited and engaged. Secretly naturally, but it had come out that he went around with a photograph and a

pressed flower in his wallet, and that he used to meet the postman far down the highway. Letta's father had taken him into
the office, talked with him for a long time, pointed out what a
serious thing an engagement is, nothing for a green new graduate. Green, that was probably a good description of him.
Anyway, his fiancée's father was nothing but a shoemaker, said
Letta. She thought the cousin's parents had been alerted.

"Imagine, engaged. Him!"

The child stood there and felt something strange in her
face, felt herself grow pale. Not red at any rate, because then
you got hot. This was a cold feeling.

"Well, good-bye," she said.

"Didn't you come to stay?"

The child was already gone, was out on the road, the good
old road with the two curves like an *S*, with thin young trees
along it and grass between the wheel tracks. Here was the
same sense of escape as always; here you could run, not only
in fantasy, but also free from all shame, everything deceitful
that was out after you. And that was over now.

For it was over right away. In a short painful moment—as
when a tooth is pulled out.

Follow the roads, never become what they call grown-up,
never what they call old, two degrading conditions that made people stupid, ugly, boring. Stay how you are now, light as a feather,
never tired, never out of breath. It came down to being careful,
not just for lengthened skirts, but also for anything like this.

For a moment the child stopped, fished out of her pocket
a dried four-leaf clover, tore it in pieces, and let the wind take
the bits.

And then she ran on, over the farmyard, right up the path
to the hill, where the fresh breeze blew.

—TRANSLATED BY BARBARA WILSON

HANDS

Xiao Hong

CHINA

Never had any of us in the school seen hands the likes of hers before: blue, black, and even showing a touch of purple, the discoloring ran from her finger tips all the way to her wrists.

We called her "The Freak" the first few days she was here. After class we always crowded around her, but not one of us had ever asked her about her hands.

Try though we might, when our teacher took roll call, we just could not keep from bursting out laughing:

"Li Jie!"

"Present."

"Zhand Zhufang!"

"Present."

"Xu Guizhen!"

"Present."

One after another in rapid, orderly fashion, we stood up as our names were called, then sat back down. But when it came Wang Yaming's turn, the process lengthened considerably.

"Hey, Wang Yaming! She's calling your name!" One of us often had to prod her before she finally stood up, her blackened hands hanging stiffly at her sides, her shoulders drooping:

Staring at the ceiling, she would answer: "Pre-se-nt!"

No matter how the rest of us laughed at her, she would never lose her composure but merely push her chair back noisily with a solemn air and sit down after what seemed like several moments. Once, at the beginning of English class, our English teacher was laughing so hard she had to remove her glasses and wipe her eyes.

"Next time you need not answer *hay-er*," she commented. "Just say 'present' in Chinese."

We were all laughing and scuffling our feet on the floor. But on the following day in English class, when Wang Yaming's name was called we were once again treated to sounds of *"Hay-er, hay-er."*

"Have you ever studied English before?" the English teacher asked as she adjusted her glasses slightly.

"You mean the language they speak in England? Sure, I've studied some, from the pock-marked teacher. Let's see, I know that they write with a *punsell* or a *pun*, but I never heard *hay-er* before."

" 'Here' simply means 'present.' It's pronounced 'here,' 'h-e-r-e.' "

"She-er, she-er." And so she began saying *she-er*. Her quaint pronunciation made everyone in the room laugh so hard we literally shook. All, that is, except Wang Yaming, who sat down very calmly and opened her book with her blackened hands. Then she began reading in a very soft voice: *"Who-at . . . deez . . . ahar . . ."**

During math class she read her formulas the same way she read essays: "$2x+y= . . . x2= . . .$"

At the lunch table, as she reached out to grab a *mantou***

---

*What . . . these . . . are. . ."

**mantou. Chinese steamed bread.

with a blackened hand, she was still occupied with her geography lesson: "Mexico produces silver . . . Yunnan . . . hmmm, Yunnan produces marble."

At night she hid herself in the bathroom and studied her lessons, and at the crack of dawn she could be found sitting at the foot of the stairs. Wherever there was the slightest glimmer of light, that's where I usually found her. One morning during a heavy snowfall, when the trees outside the window were covered with a velvety layer of white, I thought I spotted someone sleeping on the ledge of the window at the far end of the corridor in our dormitory.

"Who's there? It's so cold there!" The slapping of my shoes on the wooden floor produced a hollow sound. Since it was a Sunday morning, there was a pronounced stillness throughout the school; some of the girls were getting ready to go out, while others were still in bed asleep. Even before I had drawn up next to her I noticed the pages of the open book on her lap turning over in the wind. "Who do we have here? How can anybody be studying so hard on a Sunday!" Just as I was about to wake the girl up a pair of blackened hands suddenly caught my eye. "Wang Yaming! Hey, come on, wake up now!" This was the first time I had ever called her name, and it gave me a strange, awkward feeling.

"*Haw-haw* . . . I must have fallen asleep!"

Every time she spoke she prefaced her remarks with a dull-witted laugh.

"*Who-at . . . deez . . . yoou . . . ai,*" she began to read before she had even found her place in the book.

"*Who-at . . . deez . . .* this English is sure hard. It's nothing like our Chinese characters with radicals and the like. No, all it has is a lot of squiggles, like a bunch of worms crawling around in my brain, getting me more confused all the time, until I can't remember any more. Our English teacher says it isn't hard—

not hard, she says. Well, maybe not for the rest of you. But me, I'm stupid; we country folk just aren't as quick-witted as the rest of you. And my father's even worse off than me. He said that when he was young he only learned one character—our name Wang—and he couldn't even remember that one for more than a few minutes. *Yoou . . . ai . . . yoou . . . ah-ar . . .*" Finishing what she had to say, she tacked on a series of unrelated words from her lesson.

The ventilator on the wall whirred in the wind, as snowflakes were blown in through the window, where they stuck and turned into beads of ice. Her eyes were all bloodshot; like her blackened hands, they were greedily striving for a goal that was forever just beyond reach. In the corners of rooms or any place where even a glimmer of light remained, we saw her, looking very much like a mouse gnawing away at something.

The first time her father came to visit her he said she had gained weight: "I'll be damned, you've put on a few pounds. The chow here must be better'n it is at home, ain't that right? You keep working hard! You study here for three years or so, and even though you won't turn into no sage, at least you'll know a little somethin' about the world."

For a solid week after his visit we had a great time mimicking him. The second time he came she asked him for a pair of gloves.

"Here, you can have this pair of mine! Since you're studyin' your lessons so hard, you oughta at least have a pair of gloves. Here, don't you worry none about it. If you want some gloves, then go ahead and wear these. It's comin' on spring now, and I don't go out much anyway. Little Ming, we'll just buy another pair next winter, won't we, Little Ming?" He was standing in the doorway of the reception room bellowing, and a crowd of his daughter's classmates had gathered around him.

He continued calling out "Little Ming this" and "Little Ming that," then gave her some news from home: "Third Sister went visitin' over to Second Auntie's and stayed for two or three days! Our little pig has been gettin' a couple extra handfuls of beans every day, and he's so fat now you've never seen the like. His ears are standin' straight up. Your elder sister came home and pickled two more jars of scallions."

He was talking so much he had worked up a sweat, and just then the school principal threaded her way through the crowd of onlookers and walked up to him: "Won't you please come into the reception room and have a seat?"

"No thanks, there's no need for that, that'll just waste everyone's time. Besides, I couldn't if I wanted to; I have to go catch a train back home. All those kids at home, I don't feel right leavin' 'em there." He took his cap off and held it in his hands, then he nodded to the principal. Steam rose from his head as he pushed the door open and strode out, looking as though he had been chased off by the principal. But he stopped in his tracks and turned around, then began removing his gloves.

"Daddy, you keep them. I don't need to wear gloves anyway."

Her father's hands were also discolored, but they were both bigger and blacker than Wang Yaming's.

Later, when we were in the reading room, Wang Yaming asked me: "Tell me, is it true? If someone goes into the reception room to sit and chat, does it cost them anything?"

"Cost anything! For what?"

"Not so loud; if the others hear you, they'll start laughing at me again." She placed the palm of her hand on top of the newspaper I was reading and continued: "My father said so. He said there was a teapot and some cups in the reception room, and that if he went inside the custodian would probably pour tea, and that he would have to pay for it. I said he wasn't expected to, but he wouldn't believe me, and he said that even in a small teahouse, if you went in and just had a cup of water you'd have to pay something. It was even more likely in a school; he said, 'Just think how big a school is!' "

The principal said to her, as she had several times in the past: "Can't you wash those hands of yours clean? Use a little more soap! Wash them good and hard with hot water. During morning calisthenics out on the playground there are several hundred white hands up in the air—all but yours; no, yours are special, very special!" The principal reached out her bloodless, fossil-like transparent fingers and touched Wang Yaming's blackened hands. Holding her breath somewhat fearfully, she looked as though she were reaching out to pick up a dead crow. "They're a lot less stained than they used to be—I can even see the skin on the palms now. They're much better than they were when you first got here—they were like hands of iron then! Are you keeping up with your lessons? I want you to work a little harder, and from now on you don't have to take part in morning calisthenics. Our school wall is low, and there are a lot of foreigners strolling by on spring days who stop to take a look. You can join in again when the discoloring on your hands is all gone!" This lecture by the school principal was to bring an end to her morning calisthenics.

"I already asked my father for a pair of gloves. No one would notice them if I had gloves on, would they?" She opened up her book bag and took out the gloves her father had given her.

The principal laughed so hard at this she fell into a fit of coughing. Her pallid face suddenly reddened: "What possible good would that do? What we want is uniformity, and even if you wore gloves you still wouldn't be like the others."

The snow atop the artificial hill had melted, the bell being rung by the school custodian produced a crisper sound than usual, sprouts began to appear on the willow trees in front of the window, and a layer of steam rose from the playground under the rays of the sun. As morning calisthenics began, the sound of the exercise leader's whistle carried far into the distance; its echo reverberated among the people in the clump of trees outside the windows. We ran and jumped like a flock of noisy birds, intoxicated by the sweet fragrance that drifted over from the new buds on the branches of the trees. Our spirits, which had been imprisoned by the winter weather, were set free anew, like cotton wadding that has just been released.

As the morning calisthenics period was coming to an end we suddenly heard someone calling to us from an upstairs window in a voice that seemed to be floating up to the sky: "Just feel how warm the sun is! Aren't you hot down there? Aren't you . . ."

There standing in the window behind the budding willows was Wang Yaming.

By the time the trees were covered with green leaves and were casting their shade all over the compound, a change had come over Wang Yaming—she had begun to languish and black circles had appeared around her eyes. Her ears seemed less full than before and her strong shoulders began to slump. On one of the rare occasions when I saw her under one of the shade trees I noticed her slightly hollow chest and was reminded of someone suffering from consumption.

"The principal says my schoolwork's lagging behind, and she's right, of course; if it hasn't improved by the end of the year, well . . . *Haw-haw!* Do you think she'll really keep me back a year?" Even though her speech was still punctuated with that *haw-haw*, I could see that she was trying to hide her hands—she kept the left one behind her back, while all I could see of the right one was a lump under the sleeve of her jacket.

We had never seen her cry before, but one gusty day when the branches of the trees outside the windows were bending in the wind, she stood there with her back to the classroom and to the rest of us and wept to the wind outside. This occurred after a group of visitors had departed, and she stood there wiping the tears from her eyes with darkened hands that had already lost a good deal of their color.

"Are you crying? How dare you cry! Why didn't you go away and hide when all the visitors were here? Just look at yourself. You're the only 'special case' in the whole group! Even if I were to forget for the moment those two blue hands of yours, just look at your uniform—it's almost gray! Everybody else has on a blue blouse, but you, you're special. It doesn't look good to have someone wearing clothes so old that the color has faded. We can't let our system of uniforms go out the window because of you alone." With her lips opening and closing, the principal reached out with her pale white fingers and clutched at Wang Yaming's collar: "I told you to go downstairs and not come back up until after the visitors had left! Who told you to stand out there in the corridor? Did you really think they wouldn't see you out there? And to top it all, you had on this pair of oversized gloves."

As she mentioned the word *gloves* the principal kicked the glove that had dropped to the floor with the shiny toe of her patent shoe and said: "I suppose you figured everything would be just fine if you stood out there wearing a pair of gloves, didn't you? What kind of nonsense is that?" She kicked the glove again, but this time, looking at that huge glove, which was large enough for a carter to wear, she couldn't suppress a chuckle.

How Wang Yaming cried that time; she was still weeping even after the sounds of the wind had died down.

She returned to the school after summer vacation. The

late summer weather was as cool and brisk as autumn, and the setting sun turned the cobbled road a deep red. We had gathered beneath the crab-apple tree by the school entrance and were eating crab-apples when a horsecart from Mount Lama carrying Wang Yaming rumbled up. In the silence following the arrival of the cart her father began taking her luggage down for her, while she held onto her small washbasin and a few odds and ends. We didn't immediately make way for her when she reached the step of the gate. Some of us called out to her: "So here you are! You've come back!" Others just stood there gaping at her. As her father followed her up to the steps, the white towel which hung from his waistband flapping to and fro, someone said: "What's this? After spending a summer at home, her hands are as black as they were before. Don't they look like they're made of iron?"

I didn't really pay much attention to her ironlike hands until our post-autumn moving day. Although I was half asleep, I could hear some quarreling in the next room:

"I don't want her. I won't have my bed next to hers!"

"I don't want mine next to hers either."

I tried listening more attentively, but I couldn't hear clearly what was going on. All I could hear was some muffled laughter and an occasional sound of commotion. But going out into the corridor that night to get a drink of water, I saw someone sleeping on one of the benches. I recognized her at once—it was Wang Yaming. Her face was covered with those two blackened hands, and her quilt had slid down so that half was on the ground and the other half barely covered her legs. I thought that she was getting in some studying by the corridor light, but I saw no books beside her. There was only a clutter of personal belongings and odds and ends on the floor all around her.

On the next day the principal, followed closely by Wang Yaming, made her way among the neatly arranged beds, snorting as she did so and testing the freshly tucked bedsheets with her delicate fingers.

"Why, here's a row of seven beds with only eight girls sleeping on them; some of the others have nine girls sleeping in six beds!" As she said this she took one of the quilts and moved it slightly to one side, telling Wang Yaming to place her bedding there.

Wang Yaming opened up her bedding and whistled contentedly as she made up the bed. This was the first time I had ever heard anyone whistle in a girls' school. After she made up the bed she sat on it, her mouth open and her chin tilted slightly higher than usual, as though she were calmed by a feeling of repose and a sense of contentment. The principal had already turned and gone downstairs, and was perhaps by then out of the dormitory altogether and on her way home. But the old housemother with lackluster hair kept shuffling back and forth, scraping her shoes on the floor.

"As far as I'm concerned," she said, "this won't do at all. It's unsanitary. Who wants to be with her, with those vermin all over her body?" As she took a few steps toward the corner of the room, she seemed to be staring straight at me: "Take a look at that bedding! Have a sniff at it! You can smell the odor two feet away. Just imagine how ludicrous it is to have to sleep next to her! Who knows, those vermin of hers might hop all over anyone next to her. Look at this, have you ever seen cotton wadding as filthy as that?"

The housemother often told us stories about how she had accompanied her husband when he went overseas to study in Japan, and how she should be considered an overseas student also. When asked by some of the girls: "What did you study?" she would respond: "Why study any particular subject? I picked up some Japanese and noticed some Japanese customs while I was there. Isn't that studying abroad?" Her speech was forever dotted with terms like "unsanitary," "ludicrous," "filthy," and so on, and she always called lice "vermin."

"If someone's filthy the hands show it." When she said the word *filthy* she shrugged her broad shoulders, as though she had been struck by a blast of cold air, then suddenly darted outside.

"This kind of student! Really, the principal shouldn't have . . ." Even after the lights-out bell had sounded the housemother could still be heard talking with some of the girls in the corridor.

On the third night Wang Yaming, bundle in hand and carrying her bedding, was again walking along behind the white-faced principal.

"We don't want her. We already have enough girls here."

They started yelling before the principal had even laid a finger on their bedding, and the same thing happened when she moved on to the next row of beds.

"We're too crowded here already! Do you expect us to take any more? Nine girls on six beds; how are we supposed to take any more?"

"One, two, three, four . . ." the principal counted. "Not enough; you can still add one more. There should be six girls for every four beds, but you only have five. Come on over here, Wang Yaming!"

"No, my sister's coming tomorrow, and we're saving that space for her," one of the girls said as she ran over and held her bedding in place.

Eventually the principal led her over to another dormitory.

"She's got lice, I'm not going to sleep next to her."

"I'm not going to either."

"Wang Yaming's bedding doesn't have a cover and she sleeps right next to the cotton wadding. If you don't believe me, just look for yourself!"

Then they began to joke about it, saying they were all

afraid of Wang Yaming's black hands and didn't dare get close to her.

Finally the black-handed girl had to sleep on a bench in the corridor. On mornings when I got up early I met her there rolling up her bedding and carrying it downstairs. Sometimes I ran into her in the basement storage room. Naturally, that was always at nighttime, so when we talked I kept looking at the shadows cast on the wall; the shadows of her hands as she scratched her head were the same color as her black hair.

"Once you get used to it, you can sleep on a bench or even on the floor. After all, sleep is sleep no matter where you lie down, so what's the difference? Studying is what matters. I wonder what sort of grade Mrs. Ma is going to give me in English on our next exam. If I don't score at least sixty I'll be kept back at the end of the year, won't I?"

"Don't worry about that; they won't keep you back just because of one subject," I assured her.

"But Daddy told me I only have three years to graduate in. He said he won't be able to handle the tuition for even one extra semester. But this English language—I just can't get my tongue right for it. *Haw-haw* . . ."

Everyone in the dormitory was disgusted with her, even though she was sleeping in the corridor, because she was always coughing during the night. Another reason was that she had begun to dye her socks and blouses right in the dormitory.

"When clothes get old, if you dye them they're as good as new. Like, if you take a summer uniform and dye it gray, then you can use it as an autumn uniform. You can dye a pair of white socks black, then . . ."

"Why don't you just buy a pair of black socks?" I asked her.

"You mean those sold in the stores? When they dye them they use too much alum, so not only don't they hold up, but they tear as soon as you put them on. It's a lot better to dye them yourself. Socks are so expensive it just won't do to throw them away as soon as they have holes in them."

One Saturday night some of the girls cooked some eggs in a small iron pot, something they did nearly every Saturday, as they wanted to have something special to eat. I saw the eggs they cooked this time when they took them out of the pot. They were black, looking to me as if they had been poisoned or something. The girl who carried the eggs in roared so loudly her glasses nearly fell off: "All right, who did it! Who? Who did this!?"

Wang Yaming looked over at the girl as she squeezed her way through the others into the kitchen. After a few *haw-haws* she said: "It was me. I didn't know anyone was going to use this pot, so I dyed two pairs of socks in it. *Haw-haw* . . . I'll go and . . ."

"You'll go and do what?"

"I'll go and wash it."

"You think we'd cook eggs in the same pot you used to dye your stinky old socks! Who wants it?" The iron pot was hurled to the floor, where it clanged in front of us. Scowling, the girl wearing glasses then flung the blackened eggs to the floor as though she were throwing stones.

After everyone else had left the scene, Wang Yaming picked the eggs up off the floor, saying to herself: "Hm! Why throw a perfectly good iron pot away just because I dyed a couple of pairs of socks in it? Besides, how could new socks be 'stinky'?"

On snowy winter nights the path from the school to our dormitories was completely covered by a blanket of snow. We just pushed on ahead as best we could, bumping our way along, and when we ran into a strong wind we either turned around and walked backwards or walked sideways against the wind and snow. In the mornings we had to set out again from our dormitories, and in December it got so bad that our feet were numb with the cold, even if we ran. All of this caused a lot of grumbling and complaining, and some of the girls even began calling the principal names for placing the dormitories so far from the school and for making us leave for school before dawn.

Sometimes I met Wang Yaming as I was walking alone. There would be a sparkle to the sky and the distant snow cover as we walked along together, the moon casting our shadows ahead of us. There would be no other people in sight as the wind whistled through the trees by the side of the road and windows creaked and groaned under the driving snow. Our voices had harsh sounds to them as we talked in the sub-zero weather until our lips turned as stiff and numb as our legs and we stopped talking altogether, at which time we could hear only the crunching of the snow beneath our feet. When we rang the bell at the gate our legs were so cold they felt as if they were about to fall off, and our knees were about to buckle under us.

One morning—I forget just when it was—I walked out of the dormitory with a novel I wanted to read tucked under my arm, then turned around and pulled the door shut tight behind me. I felt very ill at ease as I looked at the blurred houses off in the distance and heard the sound of the shifting snow behind me; I grew more frightened with every step. The stars gave off only a glimmer of light, and the moon either had already set or was covered by the gray, dirty-looking clouds in the sky. Every step I took seemed to add another step to the distance I had yet to go. I hoped I would meet someone along the way, but dreaded it at the same time; for on a moonless night you could hear the footsteps long before you saw anyone, until the figure suddenly appeared without warning right in front of you.

When I reached the stone steps of the school gate my heart was pounding, and I rang the door bell with a trembling hand. Just then I heard someone on the steps behind me.

"Who is it? Who's there?"

"Me! It's me."

"Were you walking behind me all the time?" It gave me quite a fright, because I hadn't heard any steps but my own on the way over.

"No, I wasn't walking behind you; I've already been here a long time. The custodian won't open the door for me. I don't know how long I've been here shouting for him."

"Didn't you ring the bell?"

"It didn't do any good, *haw-haw*. The custodian turned on the light and came to the door, then he looked out through the window. But he wouldn't open the door for me."

The light inside came on and the door opened noisily, accompanied by some angry scolding: "What's the idea of shouting at the gate at all hours of the night? You're going to wind up at the bottom of the class anyway, so why worry about it?"

"What's going on! What's that you're saying?" Before I had even finished, the custodian's manner changed completely.

"Oh, Miss Xiao, have you been waiting there long?"

Wang Yaming and I walked to the basement together; she was coughing and her face, which had grown pale and wrinkled, shivered for a few moments. With tears induced by the cold wind on her cheeks, she sat down and opened her school book.

"Why wouldn't the custodian open the door for you?" I asked.

"Who knows? He said I was too early. He told me to go on back, saying that he was only following the principal's orders."

"How long were you waiting out there?"

"Not too long. Only a short while . . . a short while. I guess about as long as it takes to eat a meal. *Haw-haw*."

She no longer studied her lessons as she had when she first arrived. Her voice was much softer now and she just muttered to herself. Her swaying shoulders slumped forward and were much narrower than they had been, while her back was no longer straight and her chest had grown hollow. I read my novel, but very softly so as not to disturb her. This was the first time I had been so considerate, and I wondered why it was only the first time. She asked me what novels I had read and whether I knew *The Romance of the Three Kingdoms*. Every once in a while she picked the book up and looked at its cover or flipped through the pages. "You and the others are so smart. You don't even have to look at your lessons and you're still not the least bit worried about exams. But not me. Sometimes I feel like taking a break and reading something else for a change, but that just doesn't work with me."

One Sunday, when the dormitory was deserted, I was reading aloud the passage in Sinclair's *The Jungle* where the young girl laborer Marija had collapsed in the snow. I gazed out at the snow-covered ground outside the window and was moved by the scene. Wang Yaming was standing right behind me, though I was unaware of it.

"Would you lend me one of the books you've already read? This snowy weather depresses me. I don't have any family around here, and there's nothing to shop for out on the street—besides, everything costs money."

"Your father hasn't been to see you for a long time, has he?" I thought she might be feeling a little homesick.

"How could he come? A round trip on the train costs two dollars, and then there'd be nobody at home."

I handed her my copy of *The Jungle*, since I had read it before.

She laughed—*haw-haw*—then patted the edge of the bed a couple of times and began examining the cover of the book.

After she walked out of the room, I could hear her in the corridor reading the first sentence of the book loudly just as I had been doing.

One day sometime after that—again I forget just when it was, but it must have been another holiday—the dormitory was deserted all day long, right up to the time that moonlight streamed in through the windows, and the whole place was extremely lonely. I heard a rustling sound from the end of the bed, as though someone were there groping around for something. Raising my head to take a look, I noticed Wang Yaming's blackened hands in the moonlight. She was placing the book she had borrowed beside me.

"Did you like it?" I asked her. "How was it?"

At first she didn't answer me; then, covering her face with her hands and trembling, she said: "Fine."

Her voice was quivering. I sat up in bed, but she moved away, her face still buried in hands as black as the hair on her head. The long corridor was completely deserted, and my eyes were fixed on the cracks in the wooden floor, which were illuminated by moonlight.

"Marija is a very real person to me. You don't think she died after she collapsed in the snow, do you? She couldn't have died. Could she? The doctor knew she didn't have any money, though, so he wouldn't treat her . . . *haw-haw.*" Her high-pitched laugh brought tears to her eyes. "I went for a doctor once myself, when my mother was sick, but do you think he would come? First he wanted travel money, but I told him all our money was at home. I begged him to come with me then, because she was in a bad way. Do you think he would agree to come with me? He just stood there in the courtyard and asked me: 'What does your family do? You're dyers, aren't you?' I don't know why, but as soon as I told him we were dyers he turned and walked back inside. I waited for a while, but he didn't come back out, so I knocked on his door again. He said to me through the door: 'I won't be able to take care of your mother, now just go away!' so I went back home." She wiped her eyes again, then continued:

"From then on I had to take care of my two younger brothers and two younger sisters. Daddy used to dye the black and blue things, and my elder sister dyed the red ones. Then in the winter of the year that my elder sister was engaged her future mother-in-law came in from the countryside to stay with us. The moment she saw my elder sister she cried out: 'My God, those are the hands of a murderess!' After that, Daddy no longer let anyone dye only red things or only blue things. My hands are black, but if you look closely you can see traces of purple; my two younger sisters' hands are the same."

"Aren't your younger sisters in school?"

"No. Later on I'll teach them their lessons. Except that I don't know how well I'm doing myself, and if I don't do well then I won't even be able to face my younger sisters. The most we can earn for dyeing a bolt of cloth is thirty cents. How many bolts do you think we get a month? One article of clothing is a dime—big or small—and nearly everyone sends us overcoats. Take away the cost for fuel and for the dyes, and you can see what I mean. In order to pay my tuition they had to save every penny, even going without salt, so how could I even think of not doing my lessons? How could I?" She reached out and touched the book again.

My gaze was still fixed on the cracks in the floor, thinking to myself that her tears were much nobler than my sympathy.

One morning just before our winter holiday Wang Yaming was occupied with putting her personal belongings in order. Her luggage was already firmly bound, standing at the base of the wall. Not a soul went over to say goodbye to her. As we walked out of the dormitory, one by one, and passed by the bench that had served as Wang Yaming's bed, she smiled at each of us, at the same time casting glances through the window off into the distance. We scuffled along down the corridor, then walked downstairs and across the courtyard. As we reached the gate at the fence, Wang Yaming caught up with us, panting hard through her widely opened mouth.

"Since my father hasn't come yet, I might as well get in another hour's class work. Every hour counts," she announced to everyone present.

She worked up quite a sweat in this final hour of hers. She copied down every single word from the blackboard during the English class into a little notebook. She read them aloud as she did so and even copied down words she already knew as the teacher casually wrote them on the board. During the following hour, in geography class, she very laboriously copied down the maps the teacher had drawn on the board. She acted as though everything that went through her mind on this her final day had taken on great importance, and she was determined to let none of it pass unrecorded.

When class let out I took a look at her notebook, only to discover that she had copied it all down incorrectly. Her English words had either too few or too many letters. She obviously had a very troubled heart.

Her father still hadn't come to fetch her by nightfall, so she spread her bedding out once again on the bench. She had never before gone to bed as early as she did that night, and she slept much more peacefully than usual. Her hair was spread out over the quilt, her shoulders were relaxed, and she breathed deeply; there were no books beside her that night.

The following morning her father came as the sun was fixed atop the trembling snow-laden branches of the trees and birds had just left their nest for the day. He stopped at the head of the stairs, where he removed the pair of coarse felt boots that were hanging over his shoulders, then took a white towel from around his neck and wiped the snow and ice off his beard.

"So you flunked out, did you?" Small beads of water were formed on the stairs as the ice melted.

"No. We haven't even had exams yet. The principal told me I didn't need to take them, since I couldn't pass them anyway."

Her father just stood there at the head of the stairs staring at the wall, and not even the white towel that hung from his waist was moving. Having already carried her luggage out to the head of the stairs, Wang Yaming went back to get her personal things, her washbasin, and some odds and ends. She handed the large pair of gloves back to her father.

"I don't want them, you go ahead and wear them!" With each step in his coarse felt boots, he left a muddy imprint on the wooden floor.

Since it was still early in the morning, few students were there looking on as Wang Yaming put the gloves on with a weak little laugh.

"Put on your felt boots! You've already made a mess of your schooling, now don't go and freeze your feet off too," her father said as he loosened the laces of the boots, which had been tied together.

The boots reached up past her knees. Like a carter, she fastened a white scarf around her head. "I'll be back; I'll take my books home and study hard, then I'll be back. *Haw . . . haw*," she announced to no one in particular. Then as she picked up her belongings she asked her father: "Did you leave the horsecart you hired outside the gate?"

"Horsecart? What horsecart? We're gonna walk to the station. I'll carry the luggage on my back."

Wang Yaming's felt boots made slapping noises as she walked down the stairs. Her father walked ahead of her, gripping her luggage with his discolored hands. Beneath the morning sun long quivering shadows stretched out in front of them as they walked up the steps of the gate. Watched from the window, they seemed as light and airy as their own shadows; I could still see them, but I could no longer hear the sounds of their departure. After passing through the gate they headed off into the distance, in the direction of the hazy morning sun.

The snow looked like shards of broken glass, and the further the distance the stronger the reflection grew. I kept looking until the glare from the snowy landscape hurt my eyes.

—TRANSLATED BY HOWARD GOLDBLATT

CHRISTMAS MORNING

Frank O'Connor

IRELAND

I never really liked my brother, Sonny. From the time he was a baby he was always the mother's pet and always chasing her to tell her what mischief I was up to. Mind you, I was usually up to something. Until I was nine or ten I was never much good at school, and I really believe it was to spite me that he was so smart at his books. He seemed to know by instinct that this was what Mother had set her heart on, and you might almost say he spelt himself into her favor.

"Mummy," he'd say, "will I call Larry in to his t-e-a?" or: "Mummy, the k-e-t-e-l is boiling," and, of course, when he was wrong she'd correct him, and next time he'd have it right and there would be no standing him. "Mummy," he'd say, "aren't I a good speller?" Cripes, we could all be good spellers if we went on like that!

Mind you, it wasn't that I was stupid. Far from it. I was just restless and not able to fix my mind for long on any one thing. I'd do the lessons for the year before, or the lessons for the year after: what I couldn't stand were the lessons we were supposed to be doing at the time. In the evenings I used to go out and play with the Doherty gang. Not, again, that I was rough, but I liked the excitement, and for the life of me I couldn't see what attracted Mother about education.

"Can't you do your lessons first and play after?" she'd say, getting white with indignation. "You ought to be ashamed of yourself that your baby brother can read better than you."

She didn't seem to understand that I wasn't, because there didn't seem to me to be anything particularly praiseworthy about reading, and it struck me as an occupation better suited to a sissy kid like Sonny.

"The dear knows what will become of you," she'd say. "If only you'd stick to your books you might be something good like a clerk or an engineer."

"I'll be a clerk, Mummy," Sonny would say smugly.

"Who wants to be an old clerk?" I'd say, just to annoy him. "I'm going to be a soldier."

"The dear knows, I'm afraid that's all you'll ever be fit for," she would add with a sigh.

I couldn't help feeling at times that she wasn't all there. As if there was anything better a fellow could be!

Coming on to Christmas, with the days getting shorter and the shopping crowds bigger, I began to think of all the things I might get from Santa Claus. The Dohertys said there was no Santa Claus, only what your father and mother gave you, but the Dohertys were a rough class of children you wouldn't expect Santa to come to anyway. I was rooting round for whatever information I could pick up about him, but there didn't seem to be much. I was no hand with a pen, but if a letter would do any good I was ready to chance writing to him. I had plenty of initiative and was always writing off for free samples and prospectuses.

"Ah, I don't know will he come at all this year," Mother said with a worried air. "He has enough to do looking after steady boys who mind their lessons without bothering about the rest."

"He only comes to good spellers, Mummy," said Sonny. "Isn't that right?"

"He comes to any little boy who does his best, whether he's a good speller or not," Mother said firmly.

Well, I did my best. God knows I did!. It wasn't my fault if, four days before the holidays, Flogger Dawley gave us sums we couldn't do, and Peter Doherty and myself had to go on the lang.* It wasn't for love of it, for, take it from me, December is no month for mitching,** and we spent most of our time sheltering from the rain in a store on the quays. The only mistake we made was imagining we could keep it up till the holidays without being spotted. That showed real lack of foresight.

Of course, Flogger Dawley noticed and sent home word to know what was keeping me. When I came in on the third day the mother gave me a look I'll never forget, and said: "Your dinner is there." She was too full to talk. When I tried to explain to her about Flogger Dawley and the sums she brushed it aside and said: "You have no word." I saw then it wasn't the langing she minded but the lies, though I still didn't see how you could lang without lying. She didn't speak to me for days. And even then I couldn't make out what she saw in education, or why she wouldn't let me grow up naturally like anyone else.

To make things worse, it stuffed Sonny up more than ever. He had the air of one saying: "I don't know what they'd do without me in this blooming house." He stood at the front door, leaning against the jamb with his hands in his trouser pockets, trying to make himself look like Father, and shouted to the other kids so that he could be heard all over the road.

"Larry isn't left go out. He went on the lang with Peter

---

*go on the lang: to play hookey, skip school

**mitching: playing hookey

Doherty and me mother isn't talking to him."

And at night, when we were in bed, he kept it up.

"Santa Claus won't bring you anything this year, aha!"

"Of course he will," I said.

"How do you know?"

"Why wouldn't he?"

"Because you went on the lang with Doherty. I wouldn't play with them Doherty fellows."

"You wouldn't be left."

"I wouldn't play with them. They're no class. They had the bobbies up to the house."

"And how would Santa know I was on the lang with Peter Doherty?" I growled, losing patience with the little prig.

"Of course he'd know. Mummy would tell him."

"And how could Mummy tell him and he up at the North Pole? Poor Ireland, she's rearing them yet! 'Tis easy seen you're only an old baby."

"I'm not a baby, and I can spell better than you, and Santa won't bring you anything."

"We'll see whether he will or not," I said sarcastically, doing the old man on him.

But, to tell the God's truth, the old man was only bluff. You could never tell what powers these superhuman chaps would have of knowing what you were up to. And I had a bad conscience about the langing because I'd never before seen the mother like that.

That was the night I decided that the only sensible thing to do was to see Santa myself and explain to him. Being a man, he'd probably understand. In those days I was a good-looking kid and had a way with me when I liked. I had only to smile nicely at one old gent on the North Mall to get a penny from him, and I felt if only I could get Santa by himself I could do the same with him and maybe get something worth while from

him. I wanted a model railway: I was sick of Ludo and Snakes-
and-Ladders.

I started to practice lying awake, counting five hundred
and then a thousand, and trying to hear first eleven, then midnight, from Shandon. I felt sure Santa would be round by
midnight, seeing that he'd be coming from the north, and
would have the whole of the South Side to do afterwards. In
some ways I was very farsighted. The only trouble was the
things I was farsighted about.

I was so wrapped up in my own calculations that I had little attention to spare for Mother's difficulties. Sonny and I used
to go to town with her, and while she was shopping we stood
outside a toyshop in the North Main Street, arguing about what
we'd like for Christmas.

On Christmas Eve when Father came home from work
and gave her the housekeeping money, she stood looking at it
doubtfully while her face grew white.

"Well?" he snapped, getting angry. "What's wrong with
that?"

"What's wrong with it?" she muttered. "On Christmas
Eve!"

"Well," he asked truculently, sticking his hands in his
trouser pockets as though to guard what was left, "do you
think I get more because it's Christmas?"

"Lord God," she muttered distractedly. "And not a bit of
cake in the house, nor a candle, nor anything!"

"All right," he shouted, beginning to stamp. "How much
will the candle be?"

"Ah, for pity's sake," she cried, "will you give me the
money and not argue like that before the children? Do you
think I'll leave them with nothing on the one day of the year?"

"Bad luck to you and your children!" he snarled. "Am I to
be slaving from one year's end to another for you to be throwing

it away on toys? Here," he added, tossing two half-crowns on the table, "that's all you're going to get, so make the most of it."

"I suppose the publicans will get the rest," she said bitterly.

Later she went into town, but did not bring us with her, and returned with a lot of parcels, including the Christmas candle. We waited for Father to come home to his tea, but he didn't, so we had our own tea and a slice of Christmas cake each, and then Mother put Sonny on a chair with the holy-water stoup to sprinkle the candle, and when he lit it she said: "The light of heaven to our souls." I could see she was upset because Father wasn't in—it should be the oldest and youngest. When we hung up our stockings at bedtime he was still out.

Then began the hardest couple of hours I ever put in. I was mad with sleep but afraid of losing the model railway, so I lay for a while, making up things to say to Santa when he came. They varied in tone from frivolous to grave, for some old gents like kids to be modest and well-spoken, while others prefer them with spirit. When I had rehearsed them all I tried to wake Sonny to keep me company, but that kid slept like the dead.

Eleven struck from Shandon, and soon after I heard the latch, but it was only Father coming home.

"Hello, little girl," he said, letting on to be surprised at finding Mother waiting up for him, and then broke into a self-conscious giggle. "What have you up so late?"

"Do you want your supper?" she asked shortly.

"Ah, no, no," he replied. "I had a bit of pig's cheek at Daneen's on my way up (Daneen was my uncle). I'm very fond of a bit of pig's cheek. . . . My goodness, is it that late?" he exclaimed, letting on to be astonished. "If I knew that I'd have gone to the North Chapel for midnight Mass. I'd like to hear the *Adeste* again. That's a hymn I'm very fond of—a most touching hymn."

Then he began to hum it falsetto.

Adeste fideles
Solus domus dagus.

Father was very fond of Latin hymns, particularly when
he had a drop in, but as he had no notion of the words he made
them up as he went along, and this always drove Mother mad.

"Ah, you disgust me!" she said in a scalded voice, and
closed the room door behind her. Father laughed as if he
thought it a great joke; and he struck a match to light his pipe
and for a while puffed at it noisily. The light under the door
dimmed and went out but he continued to sing emotionally.

Dixie medearo
Tutum tonum tantum
Venite adoremus.

He had it all wrong but the effect was the same on me. To
save my life I couldn't keep awake.

Coming on to dawn, I woke with the feeling that something dreadful had happened. The whole house was quiet, and
the little bedroom that looked out on the foot and a half of back
yard was pitch-dark. It was only when I glanced at the window
that I saw how all the silver had drained out of the sky. I jumped
out of bed to feel my stocking, well knowing that the worst had
happened. Santa had come while I was asleep, and gone away
with an entirely false impression of me, because all he had left
me was some sort of book, folded up, a pen and pencil, and a
tuppenny bag of sweets. Not even Snakes-and-Ladders! For a
while I was too stunned even to think. A fellow who was able to
drive over rooftops and climb down chimneys without getting
stuck—God, wouldn't you think he'd know better?

Then I began to wonder what that foxy boy, Sonny, had. I went to his side of the bed and felt his stocking. For all his spelling and sucking-up he hadn't done so much better, because, apart from a bag of sweets like mine, all Santa had left him was a popgun, one that fired a cork on a piece of string and which you could get in any huxter's shop for sixpence.

All the same, the fact remained that it was a gun, and a gun was better than a book any day of the week. The Dohertys had a gang, and the gang fought the Strawberry Lane kids who tried to play football on our road. That gun would be very useful to me in many ways, while it would be lost on Sonny who wouldn't be let play with the gang, even if he wanted to.

Then I got the inspiration, as it seemed to me, direct from heaven. Suppose I took the gun and gave Sonny the book! Sonny would never be any good in the gang: he was fond of spelling, and a studious child like him could learn a lot of spellings from a book like mine. As he hadn't seen Santa any more than I had, what he hadn't seen wouldn't grieve him. I was doing no harm to anyone; in fact, if Sonny only knew, I was doing him a good turn which he might have cause to thank me for later. That was one thing I was always keen on; doing good turns. Perhaps this was Santa's intention the whole time and he had merely become confused between us. It was a mistake that might happen to anyone. So I put the book, the pencil, and the pen into Sonny's stocking and the popgun into my own, and returned to bed and slept again. As I say, in those days I had plenty of initiative.

It was Sonny who woke me, shaking me to tell me that Santa had come and left me a gun. I let on to be surprised and rather disappointed in the gun, and to divert his mind from it made him show me his picture book, and cracked it up to the skies.

As I knew, that kid was prepared to believe anything, and

nothing would do him then but to take the presents in to show Father and Mother. This was a bad moment for me. After the way she had behaved about the langing, I distrusted Mother, though I had the consolation of believing that the only person who could contradict me was now somewhere up by the North Pole. That gave me a certain confidence, so Sonny and I burst in with our presents, shouting: "Look what Santa Claus brought!"

Father and Mother woke, and Mother smiled, but only for an instant. As she looked at me her face changed. I knew that look; I knew it only too well. It was the same she had worn the day I came home from langing, when she said I had no word.

"Larry," she said in a low voice, "where did you get that gun?"

"Santa left it in my stocking, Mummy," I said, trying to put on an injured air, though it baffled me how she guessed that he hadn't. "He did, honest."

"You stole it from that poor child's stocking while he was asleep," she said, her voice quivering with indignation. "Larry, Larry, how could you be so mean?"

"Now, now, now," Father said deprecatingly, "'tis Christmas morning."

"Ah," she said with real passion, "it's easy it comes to you. Do you think I want my son to grow up a liar and a thief?"

"Ah, what thief, woman?" he said testily. "Have sense, can't you?" He was as cross if you interrupted him in his benevolent moods as if they were of the other sort, and this one was probably exacerbated by a feeling of guilt for his behavior of the night before. "Here, Larry," he said, reaching out for the money on the bedside table, "here's sixpence for you and one for Sonny. Mind you don't lose it now."

But I looked at Mother and saw what was in her eyes. I burst out crying, threw the popgun on the floor, and ran bawling out of the house before anyone on the road was awake. I rushed up the lane behind the house and threw myself on the wet grass.

I understood it all, and it was almost more than I could bear; that there was no Santa Claus, as the Dohertys said, only Mother trying to scrape together a few coppers from the house-keeping; that Father was mean and common and a drunkard, and that she had been relying on me to raise her out of the mis-ery of the life she was leading. And l knew that the look in her eyes was the fear that, like my father, I should turn out to be mean and common and a drunkard.

A WALK TO THE JETTY

Jamaica Kincaid

ANTIGUA

"My name is Annie John." These were the first words that
came into my mind as I woke up on the morning of the
last day I spent in Antigua, and they stayed there, lined up one
behind the other, marching up and down, for I don't know how
long. At noon on that day, a ship on which I was to be a passen-
ger would sail to Barbados, and there I would board another
ship, which would sail to England, where I would study to
become a nurse. My name was the last thing I saw the night
before, just as I was falling asleep; it was written in big, black
letters all over my trunk, sometimes followed by my address in
Antigua, sometimes followed by my address as it would be in
England. I did not want to go to England, I did not want to be a
nurse, but I would have chosen going off to live in a cavern and
keeping house for seven unruly men rather than go on with my
life as it stood. I never wanted to lie in this bed again, my legs
hanging out way past the foot of it, tossing and turning on my
mattress, with its cotton stuffing all lumped just where it was-
n't a good place to be lumped. I never wanted to lie in my bed
again and hear Mr. Ephraim driving his sheep to pasture—a sig-
nal to my mother that she should get up to prepare my father's
and my bath and breakfast. I never wanted to lie in my bed and

hear her get dressed, washing her face, brushing her teeth, and gargling. I especially never wanted to lie in my bed and hear my mother gargling again.

Lying there in the half-dark of my room, I could see my shelf, with my books—some of them prizes I had won in school, some of them gifts from my mother—and with photographs of people I was supposed to love forever no matter what, and with my old thermos, which was given to me for my eighth birthday, and some shells I had gathered at different times I spent at the sea. In one corner stood my washstand and its beautiful basin of white enamel with blooming red hibiscus painted at the bottom and an urn that matched. In another corner were my old school shoes and my Sunday shoes. In still another corner, a bureau held my old clothes. I knew everything in this room, inside out and outside in. I had lived in this room for thirteen of my seventeen years. I could see in my mind's eye even the day my father was adding it onto the rest of the house. Everywhere I looked stood something that had meant a lot to me, that had given me pleasure at some point, or could remind me of a time that was a happy time. But as I was lying there my heart could have burst open with joy at the thought of never having to see any of it again.

If someone had asked me for a little summing up of my life at that moment as I lay in bed, I would have said, "My name is Annie John. I was born on the fifteenth of September, seventeen years ago, at Holberton Hospital, at five o'clock in the morning. At the time I was born, the moon was going down at one end of the sky and the sun was coming up at the other. My mother's name is Annie also. My father's name is Alexander, and he is thirty-five years older than my mother. Two of his children are four and six years older than she is. Looking at how sickly he has become and looking at the way my mother now has to run up and down for him, gathering the herbs and barks that he boils in water, which he drinks instead of the medicine the doctor has ordered for him, I plan not only never to marry an old man but certainly never to marry at all. The house we live in my father built with his own hands. The bed I am lying in my father built with his own hands. If I get up and sit on a chair, it is a chair my father built with his own hands. When my mother uses a large wooden spoon to stir the porridge we sometimes eat as part of our breakfast, it will be a spoon that my father has carved with his own hands. The sheets on my bed my mother made with her own hands. The curtains hanging at my window my mother made with her own hands. The nightie I am wearing, with scalloped neck and hem and sleeves, my mother made with her own hands. When I look at things in a certain way, I suppose I should say that the two of them made me with their own hands. For most of my life, when the three of us went anywhere together I stood between the two of them or sat between the two of them. But then I got too big, and there I was, shoulder to shoulder with them more or less, and it became not very comfortable to walk down the street together. And so now there they are together and here I am apart. I don't see them now the way I used to, and I don't love them now the way I used to. The bitter thing about it is that they are just the same and it is I who have changed, so all the things I used to be and all the things I used to feel are as false as the teeth in my father's head. Why, I wonder, didn't I see the hypocrite in my mother when, over the years, she said that she loved me and could hardly live without me, while at the same time proposing and arranging separation after separation, including this one, which, unbeknownst to her, *I* have arranged to be permanent? So now I, too, have hypocrisy, and breasts (small ones), and hair growing in the appropriate places, and sharp eyes, and I have made a vow never to be fooled again."

Lying in my bed for the last time, I thought, This is what I add up to. At that, I felt as if someone had placed me in a hole and was forcing me first down and then up against the pressure of gravity. I shook myself and prepared to get up. I said to myself, "I am getting up out of this bed for the last time." Everything I would do that morning until I got on the ship that would take me to England I would be doing for the last time, for I had made up my mind that, come what may, the road for me now went only in one direction: away from my home, away from my mother, away from my father, away from the everlasting blue sky, away from the everlasting hot sun, away from people who said to me, "This happened during the time your mother was carrying you." If I had been asked to put into words why I felt this way, if I had been given years to reflect and come up with the words of why I felt this way, I would not have been able to come up with so much as the letter "A." I only knew that I felt the way I did, and that this feeling was the strongest thing in my life.

The Anglican church bell struck seven. My father had already bathed and dressed and was in his workshop puttering around. As if the day of my leaving were something to celebrate, they were treating it as a holiday, and nothing in the usual way would take place. My father would not go to work at all. When I got up, my mother greeted me with a big, bright "Good morning"—so big and bright that I shrank before it. I bathed quickly in some warm bark water that my mother had prepared for me. I put on my underclothes—all of them white and all of them smelling funny. Along with my earrings, my neck chain, and my bracelets, all made of gold from British Guiana, my underclothes had been sent to my mother's obeah woman, and whatever she had done to my jewelry and underclothes would help protect me from evil spirits and every kind of misfortune. The things I never wanted to see or hear or do again now made up at least three weeks' worth of grocery lists. I placed a mark against obeah women, jewelry, and white underclothes. Over my underclothes, I put on an around-the-yard dress of my mother's. The clothes I would wear for my voyage were a dark-blue pleated skirt and a blue-and-white checked blouse (the blue in the blouse matched exactly the blue of my skirt) with a large sailor collar and with a tie made from the same material as the skirt—a blouse that came down a long way past my waist, over my skirt. They were lying on a chair, freshly ironed by my mother. Putting on my clothes was the last thing I would do just before leaving the house. Miss Cornelia came and pressed my hair and then shaped it into what felt like a hundred corkscrews, all lying flat against my head so that my hat would fit properly.

At breakfast, I was seated in my usual spot, with my mother at one end of the table, my father at the other, and me in the middle, so that as they talked to me or to each other I would shift my head to the left or to the right and get a good look at them. We were having a Sunday breakfast, a breakfast as if we had just come back from Sunday-morning services: salt fish and antroba and souse and hard-boiled eggs, and even special Sunday bread from Mr. Daniel, our baker. On Sundays, we ate this big breakfast at eleven o'clock and then we didn't eat again until four o'clock, when we had our big Sunday dinner. It was the best breakfast we ate, and the only breakfast better than that was the one we ate on Christmas morning. My parents were in a festive mood, saying what a wonderful time I would have in my new life, what a wonderful opportunity this was for me, and what a lucky person I was. They were eating away as they talked, my father's false teeth making that clop-clop sound like a horse on a walk as he talked, my mother's mouth going up and down like a donkey's as she chewed each mouthful thirty-two times. (I had long ago counted, because it was something she made me do also, and I was trying to see if this was just one of her rules that applied only to me.) I was looking at them with a smile on my face but disgust in my heart when my mother said, "Of course, you are a young lady now, and we won't be surprised if in due time you write to say that one day soon you are to be married."

Without thinking, I said, with bad feeling that I didn't hide very well, "How absurd!"

My parents immediately stopped eating and looked at me as if they had not seen me before. My father was the first to go back to his food. My mother continued to look. I don't know what went through her mind, but I could see her using her tongue to dislodge food stuck in the far corners of her mouth.

Many of my mother's friends now came to say goodbye to me, and to wish me God's blessings. I thanked them and showed the proper amount of joy at the glorious things they pointed out to me that my future held and showed the proper amount of sorrow at how much my parents and everyone else who loved me would miss me. My body ached a little at all this false going back and forth, at all this taking in of people gazing at me with heads tilted, love and pity on their smiling faces. I could have left without saying any goodbyes to them and I wouldn't have missed it. There was only one person I felt I should say goodbye to, and that was my former friend Gwen. We had long ago drifted apart, and when I saw her now my heart nearly split in two with embarrassment at the feelings I used to have for her and things I had shared with her. She had now degenerated into complete silliness, hardly able to complete a sentence without putting in a few giggles. Along with the giggles, she had developed some other schoolgirl traits that she did not have when she was actually a schoolgirl, so beneath her were such things then. When we were saying our goodbyes, it was all I could do not to say cruelly, "Why are you behaving like such a monkey?" Instead, I put everything on a friendly plain, wishing her well and the best in the future. It was then that she told me that she was more or less engaged to a boy she had known while growing up early on in Nevis, and that soon, in a year or so, they would be married. My reply to her was "Good luck," and she thought I meant her well, so she grabbed me and said, "Thank you. I knew you would be happy about it." But to me it was as if she had shown me a high point from which she was going to jump and hoped to land in one piece on her feet. We parted, and when I turned away I didn't look back.

My mother had arranged with a stevedore to take my trunk to the jetty ahead of me. At ten o'clock on the dot, I was dressed, and we set off for the jetty. An hour after that, I would board a launch that would take me out to sea, where I then would board the ship. Starting out, as if for old time's sake and without giving it a thought, we lined up in the old way: I walking between my mother and my father. I loomed way above my father and could see the top of his head. We must have made a strange sight: a grown girl all dressed up in the middle of a morning, in the middle of the week, walking in step in the middle between her two parents, for people we didn't know stared at us. It was all of half an hour's walk from our house to the jetty, but I was passing through most of the years of my life. We passed by the house where Miss Dulcie, the seamstress that I had been apprenticed to for a time, lived, and just as I was passing by, a wave of bad feeling for her came over me, because I suddenly remembered that the months I spent with her all she had me do was sweep the floor, which was always full of threads and pins and needles, and I never seemed to sweep it clean enough to please her. Then she would send me to the store to buy buttons or thread, though I was only allowed to do this if I was given a sample of the button or thread, and then she would find fault even though they were an exact match of the samples she had given me. And all the while she said to me, "A girl like you will never learn to sew properly, you know." At the time, I don't suppose I minded it, because it was customary to treat the first-year apprentice with such scorn, but now I placed on the dustheap of my life Miss Dulcie and everything that I had had to do with her.

We were soon on the road that I had taken to school, to church, to Sunday school, to choir practice, to Brownie meetings, to Girl Guide meetings, to meet a friend. I was five years old when I first walked on this road unaccompanied by someone to hold my hand. My mother had placed three pennies in my little basket, which was a duplicate of her bigger basket, and sent me to the chemist's shop to buy a pennyworth of senna leaves, a pennyworth of eucalyptus leaves, and a pennyworth of camphor. She then instructed me on what side of the road to walk, where to make a turn, where to cross, how to look carefully before I crossed, and if I met anyone that I knew to politely pass greetings and keep on my way. I was wearing a freshly ironed yellow dress that had printed on it scenes of acrobats flying through the air and swinging on a trapeze. I had just had a bath, and after it, instead of powdering me with my baby-smelling talcum powder, my mother had, as a special favor, let me use her own talcum powder, which smelled quite perfumy and came in a can that had painted on it people going out to dinner in nineteenth-century London and was called Mazie. How it pleased me to walk out the door and bend my head down to sniff at myself and see that I smelled just like my mother. I went to the chemist's shop, and he had to come from behind the counter and bend down to hear what it was that I wanted to buy, my voice was so little and timid then. I went back just the way I had come, and when I walked into the yard and presented my basket with its three packages to my mother, her eyes filled with tears and she swooped me up and held me high in the air and said that I was wonderful and good and that there would never be anybody better. If I had just conquered Persia, she couldn't have been more proud of me.

We passed by our church—the church in which I had been christened and received and had sung in the junior choir. We passed by a house in which a girl I used to like and was sure I couldn't live without had lived. Once, when she had mumps, I went to visit her against my mother's wishes, and we sat on her bed and ate the cure of roasted, buttered sweet potatoes that had been placed on her swollen jaws, held there by a piece of white cloth. I don't know how, but my mother found out about it, and I don't know how, but she put an end to our friendship. Shortly after, the girl moved with her family across the sea to somewhere else. We passed the doll store, where I would go with my mother when I was little and point out the doll I wanted that year for Christmas. We passed the store where I bought the much-fought-over shoes I wore to church to be received in. We passed the bank. On my sixth birthday, I was given, among other things, the present of a sixpence. My mother and I then went to this bank, and with the sixpence I opened my own savings account. I was given a little gray book with my name in big letters on it, and in the balance column it said "6d." Every Saturday morning after that, I was given a sixpence—later a shilling, and later a two-and-sixpence piece—and I would take it to the bank for deposit. I had never been allowed to withdraw even a farthing from my bank account until just a few weeks before I was to leave; then the whole account was closed out, and I received from the bank the sum of six pounds ten shillings and two and a half pence.

We passed the office of the doctor who told my mother

three times that I did not need glasses, that if my eyes were feeling weak a glass of carrot juice a day would make them strong again. This happened when I was eight. And so every day at recess I would run to my school gate and meet my mother, who was waiting for me with a glass of juice from carrots she had just grated and then squeezed, and I would drink it and then run back to meet my chums. I knew there was nothing at all wrong with my eyes, but I had recently read a story in *The Schoolgirl's Own Annual* in which the heroine, a girl a few years older than I was then, cut such a figure to my mind with the way she was always adjusting her small, round, horn-rimmed glasses that I felt I must have a pair exactly like them. When it became clear that I didn't need glasses, I began to complain about the glare of the sun being too much for my eyes, and I walked around with my hands shielding them—especially in my mother's presence. My mother then bought for me a pair of sunglasses with the exact horn-rimmed frames I wanted, and how I enjoyed the gestures of blowing on the lenses, wiping them with the hem of my uniform, adjusting the glasses when they slipped down my nose, and just removing them from their case and putting them on. In three weeks, I grew tired of them and they found a nice resting place in a drawer, along with some other things that at one time or another I couldn't live without.

We passed the store that sold only grooming aids, all imported from England. This store had in it a large porcelain dog—white, with black spots all over and a red ribbon of satin tied around its neck. The dog sat in front of a white porcelain bowl that was always filled with fresh water, and it sat in such a way that it looked as if it had just taken a long drink. When I was a small child, I would ask my mother, if ever we were near this store, to please take me to see the dog, and I would stand in front of it, bent over slightly, my hands resting on my knees, and stare at it and stare at it. I thought this dog more beautiful and more real than any actual dog I had ever seen or any actual dog I would ever see. I must have outgrown my interest in the dog, for when it disappeared I never asked what became of it. We passed the library, and if there was anything on this walk that I might have wept over leaving, this most surely would have been the thing. My mother had been a member of the library long before I was born. And since she took me every-where with her when I was quite little, when she went to the library she took me along there, too. I would sit in her lap very quietly as she read books that she did not want to take home with her. I could not read the words yet, but just the way they looked on the page was interesting to me. Once, a book she was reading had a large picture of a man in it, and when I asked her who he was she told me that he was Louis Pasteur and that the book was about his life. It stuck in my mind, because she said it was because of him that she boiled my milk to purify it before I was allowed to drink it, that it was his idea, and that that was why the process was called pasteurization. One of the things I had put away in my mother's old trunk in which she kept all my childhood things was my library card. At that moment, I owed sevenpence in overdue fees.

As I passed by all these places, it was as if I were in a dream, for I didn't notice the people coming and going in and out of them, I didn't feel my feet touch ground, I didn't even feel my own body—I just saw these places as if they were hanging in the air, not having top or bottom, and as if I had gone in and out of them all in the same moment. The sun was bright; the sky was blue and just above my head. We then arrived at the jetty.

My heart now beat fast, and no matter how hard I tried, I couldn't keep my mouth from falling open and my nostrils from spreading to the ends of my face. My old fear of slipping between the boards of the jetty and falling into the dark-green water where the dark-green eels lived came over me. When my father's stomach started to go bad, the doctor had recommended a walk every evening right after he ate his dinner. Sometimes he would take me with him. When he took me with him, we usually went to the jetty, and there he would sit and talk to the night watchman about cricket or some other thing that didn't interest me, because it was not personal; they didn't talk about their wives, or their children, or their parents, or about any of their likes and dislikes. They talked about things in such a strange way, and I didn't see what they found funny, but sometimes they made each other laugh so much that their guffaws would bound out to sea and send back an echo. I was always sorry when we got to the jetty and saw that the night watchman on duty was the one he enjoyed speaking to; it was like being locked up in a book filled with numbers and diagrams and what-ifs. For the thing about not being able to understand and enjoy what they were saying was I had nothing to take my mind off my fear of slipping in between the boards of the jetty.

Now, too, I had nothing to take my mind off what was happening to me. My mother and my father—I was leaving them forever. My home on an island—I was leaving it forever. What to make of everything? I felt a familiar hollow space inside. I felt I was being held down against my will. I felt I was burning up from head to toe. I felt that someone was tearing me up into little pieces and soon I would be able to see all the little pieces as they floated out into nothing in the deep blue sea. I didn't know whether to laugh or cry. I could see that it would be better not to think too clearly about any one thing. The launch was being made ready to take me, along with some other passengers, out to the ship that was anchored in the sea.

My father paid our fares, and we joined a line of people waiting
to board. My mother checked my bag to make sure that I had
my passport, the money she had given me, and a sheet of paper
placed between some pages in my Bible on which were written
the names of the relatives—people I had not known existed—
with whom I would live in England. Across from the jetty was a
wharf, and some stevedores were loading and unloading
barges. I don't know why seeing that struck me so, but suddenly a wave of strong feeling came over me, and my heart swelled
with a great gladness as the words "I shall never see this again"
spilled out inside me. But then, just as quickly, my heart shriv-
eled up and the words "I shall never see this again" stabbed at
me. I don't know what stopped me from falling in a heap at my
parents' feet.

When we were all on board, the launch headed out to sea.
Away from the jetty, the water became the customary blue, and
the launch left a wide path in it that looked like a road. I passed
by sounds and smells that were so familiar that I had long ago
stopped paying any attention to them. But now here they were,
and the ever-present "I shall never see this again" bobbed up
and down inside me. There was the sound of the seagull diving
down into the water and coming up with something silverish in
its mouth. There was the smell of the sea and the sight of small
pieces of rubbish floating around in it. There were boats filled
with fishermen coming in early. There was the sound of their
voices as they shouted greetings to each other. There was the
hot sun, there was the blue sea, there was the blue sky. Not
very far away, there was the white sand of the shore, with the
run-down houses all crowded in next to each other, for in some
places only poor people lived near the shore. I was seated in
the launch between my parents, and when I realized that I was
gripping their hands tightly I glanced quickly to see if they were
looking at me with scorn, for I felt sure that they must have

known of my never-see-this-again feelings. But instead my
father kissed me on the forehead and my mother kissed me on
the mouth, and they both gave over their hands to me, so that I
could grip them as much as I wanted. I was on the verge of
feeling that it had all been a mistake, but I remembered that I
wasn't a child anymore, and that now when I made up my mind
about something I had to see it through. At that moment, we
came to the ship, and that was that.

The goodbyes had to be quick, the captain said. My mother
introduced herself to him and then introduced me. She told
him to keep an eye on me, for I had never gone this far away
from home on my own. She gave him a letter to pass on to the
captain of the next ship that I would board in Barbados. They
walked me to my cabin, a small space that I would share with
someone else—a woman I did not know. I had never before
slept in a room with someone I did not know. My father kissed
me goodbye and told me to be good and to write home often.
After he said this, he looked at me, then looked at the floor and
swung his left foot, then looked at me again. I could see that he
wanted to say something else, something that he had never
said to me before, but then he just turned and walked away. My
mother said, "Well," and then she threw her arms around me.
Big tears streamed down her face, and it must have been that—
for I could not bear to see my mother cry—which started me
crying, too. She then tightened her arms around me and held
me to her close, so that I felt that I couldn't breathe. With that,
my tears dried up and I was suddenly on my guard. "What does
she want now?" I said to myself. Still holding me close to her,
she said, in a voice that raked across my skin, "It doesn't matter what you do or where you go, I'll always be your mother
and this will always be your home."

I dragged myself away from her and backed off a little,

and then I shook myself, as if to wake myself out of a stupor. We looked at each other for a long time with smiles on our faces, but I know the opposite of that was in my heart. As if responding to some invisible cue, we both said, at the very same moment, "Well." Then my mother turned around and walked out the cabin door. I stood there for I don't know how long, and then I remembered that it was customary to stand on deck and wave to your relatives who were returning to shore. From the deck, I could not see my father, but I could see my mother facing the ship, her eyes searching to pick me out. I removed from my bag a red cotton handkerchief that she had earlier given me for this purpose, and I waved it wildly in the air. Recognizing me immediately, she waved back just as wildly, and we continued to do this until she became just a dot in the matchbox-size launch swallowed up in the big blue sea.

I went back to my cabin and lay down on my berth. Everything trembled as if it had a spring at its very center. I could hear the small waves lap-lapping around the ship. They made an unexpected sound, as if a vessel filled with liquid had been placed on its side and now was slowly emptying out.

ABOUT THE AUTHORS

Ama Ata Aidoo was born in 1942 in Ghana. She is a poet, playwright, and fiction writer. Her first play, *Dilemma of a Ghost*, written when she was twenty-two years old, won immediate acclaim. Other well-known works include her collection of short stories, *No Sweetness Here*, all about life in Ghana, and the novels *Our Sister Killjoy* and *Changes*, which won the 1993 Commonwealth Writers Prize, Africa Division. Until 1983 Aidoo had a distinguished academic career and then held high political office as education minister.

Toni Cade Bambara was born in 1939 in New York City, where she grew up. She discovered the name *Bambara* as a signature on a sketchbook in her grandmother's trunk and added it to her original name. She began writing fiction while in college; "Sweet Town" was her first published story. It appeared in *Vendome* magazine when she was twenty years old. Bambara taught and lectured at universities throughout the United States. She edited two collections, *The Black Woman* and *Tales and Short Stories for Black Folk*, and was the author of the short story collections *Gorilla, My Love* and *The Sea Birds Are Still Alive* and the highly acclaimed novel *The Salt Eaters*. Toni Cade Bambara died in 1997. A collection of essays, *Deep Sightings and Rescue Missions*, was published posthumously.

Heinrich Böll, the novelist, poet, and short story writer known as the conscience of his age," was born in 1917 in Cologne, Ger .any, into a pacifist Catholic family. As a young man, he was drafted into the Wehrmacht during the Second World War ; .ıd served on the Russian and French fronts. After the war, he enrolled in the University of Cologne but dropped out to write about his experiences as a soldier. The cruelties and political injustices he witnessed under the Nazis formed the basis of most of his writing. Among his novels and short stories are *The Train Was On Time, Group Portrait with Lady, The Clown, The Safety Net,* and *What's to Become of the Boy?* Böll was also an outspoken defender of artistic and intellectual freedom for writers around the world. In 1972 he won the Nobel Prize for Literature. He died in 1985.

Italo Calvino, considered a modern master of allegorical writing, was born in Cuba in 1923 to Italian parents. He lived in San Remo, Rome, and Paris. His fiction ranges from classic storytelling to bold experiments with form, including the following titles: *The Castle of Crossed Destinies, Invisible Cities, Cosmicomics, t zero, The Watcher and Other Stories,* and *The Baron in the Trees.* He is also known for his compilation of Italian folk tales and his essays on the art of storytelling and writing. He died in 1985.

Anita Desai was born in 1937 in Mussoorie, India, to a Bengali father and German mother and educated in Delhi. She has written several books for children but is best known for her fiction and short stories, including *Clear Light of Day, Fire on the Mountain, In Custody, Journey to Ithaca,* and *Baumgartner's Bombay.* Her work has won many awards and been shortlisted twice for the Booker Prize. She is married and the mother of four children, and she divides her time between England and the United States.

Elizabeth Jolley was born in 1923 in England and brought up in a household "half English and three-quarters Viennese." She moved to Australia with her husband and three children in 1959. Although first trained as a nurse, she also worked as a door-to-door salesman, a real estate agent, and a flight attendant. Jolley wrote for twenty years before publishing her first novel, which, however, quickly brought her acclaim. She has written plays, poetry, short stories, and novels, including *Five Acre Virgin, Palomino, Foxybaby, The Sugar Mother, Miss Peabody's Inheritance, Mr. Scobie's Riddle, Milk and Honey, The Newspaper of Claremont Street, The Well,* and *Cabin Fever.* Jolley has won the Booker Prize and was awarded the Order of Australia for services to Australian literature. She lives with her husband, a retired university librarian, in western Australia.

Yasunari Kawabata, winner of the 1968 Nobel Prize for Literature, was the first Japanese writer to receive this honor. He was born in Osaka, Japan, in 1899. As a boy, he wanted to be a painter, but after he wrote and published his first stories in high school, he went on to become a writer. His novels include *Snow Country, Thousand Cranes, The Sound of the Mountain, The Master of Go,* and *Beauty and Sadness.* His short stories, written over a fifty-year period, were collected in *Palm-of-the-Hand Stories.* In addition to being a fiction writer, he was also a literary critic and discovered, among other writers, Yukio Mishima. In 1972, at the age of seventy-three, Kawabata committed suicide. He left no note or explanation.

Jamaica Kincaid was born Elaine Potter Richardson in 1949 on the island of St. John's, Antigua. Her mother was a homemaker and political activist, and her stepfather was a cabinetmaker and carpenter. In 1966, just after her seventeenth birthday, she left the island to work as an au pair in New York City. In 1973 she changed her name to Jamaica Kincaid and had her first publication. She is the author of highly acclaimed works of fiction and nonfiction: *Annie John, At the Bottom of the River, Lucy, A Small Place, Autobiography of My Mother,* and most recently, *My Brother.* She lives in Vermont with her family.

Naguib Mahfouz, the 1988 Nobel Prize-winner for Literature, was born in 1911 in Cairo, Egypt. The crowded Old Cairo district of al-Gamaliyya, where he spent his early childhood, is the setting of many of his novels and stories. He was the youngest of seven children of devout Muslim parents. As a child, he witnessed upheavals of war, martial law, rebellion, and the exile and return of a family hero who espoused the cause of independence from British rule. In 1930, he attended the Secular University in Cairo, where he studied philosophy. At age seventeen, he began writing; his first novel, set in ancient Egypt, was published in 1939. Mahfouz's early writing established him as a pioneer of the Arabic novel. Until his retirement in 1972, he worked in government ministries. He has written over thirty novels and more than one hundred short stories, including the three novels of *The Cairo Trilogy: Palace Walk, Palace of Desire,* and *Sugar Street;* and *The Thief and the Dogs, The Beginning and The End, Wedding Song, The Beggar,* and *Midaq Alley.* Mahfouz lives with his family in a suburb of Cairo.

Frank O'Connor (the pseudonym of Michael O'Donovan) was born in Cork in 1903 and died in Dublin in 1966. Most of his childhood and adolescence was spent in poverty, which he reflected on in his autobiography *An Only Child* and in some of his novels and short stories. During the Irish Civil War, he fought on the Republican side and was imprisoned in Gormanstown. He described this period in his first book of short stories, *Guests of the Nation*. He was active in the Irish literary revival of the thirties and forties (which included, among others, Yeats and Synge), and was also a director of the Abbey Theater and poetry editor of *The Bell*. His writing includes translations, plays, novels, criticism, autobiography, poetry, biography, and short stories. Among his published works are the short story collections *Domestic Relations*, *Bones of Contention*, *The Common Chord*, and *The Collected Stories*, as well as the novel *The Saint and Mary Kate*. In 1950, O'Connor left Ireland to teach in the United States, where his short stories won great acclaim.

V. S. (Victor Sawdon) Pritchett, whose life spanned almost the entire twentieth century, was born near London, in Ipswich, Suffolk, in 1900. His father was a traveling salesman, his mother a poor Cockney shopclerk. The family moved eighteen times from the time he was born until he was twelve. When he was not yet sixteen, his father took him out of school and sent him to work in the leather trade in London, where he stayed for four years. At age twenty, determined to become a writer, he made his escape to Paris, where he worked in the shellac, glue, and photographic trades, and nearly starved to death. Considered by many one of the greatest prose stylists in the English language, Pritchett was a short story writer, novelist, biographer, critic, and travel writer. In 1975 he was knighted for his services to literature. He died in 1997.

Valentin Rasputin was born in 1937 in the village of Ust-Uda on the Angara River in the East Siberian province of Irkutsk. He was raised by his mother and grandmother. His father, a farmer and a logger, was imprisoned during the Stalin era for loss of public funds through negligence. Rasputin's childhood was shaped by postwar famine, the collectivization of farming under Stalin, and the disappearance of traditional village life. At age eleven, his mother sent him to the county seat to finish his education. He attended the university in Irkutsk, where he intended to become a teacher. After graduation, he worked as a journalist and published his first short stories. His work, which includes short stories and novellas, is collected in *Siberia on Fire, Farewell to Matyora, You Live and Love and Other Stories, Live and Remember,* and *Money for Maria and Borrowed Time—Two Village Tales.* Rasputin and his wife live in Irkutsk and have two grown children.

Cora Sandel, whose real name was Sara Fabricus, was born in Oslo, Norway, in 1880 and died in 1974 in Sweden. Her father was a naval officer, and when she was twelve the family moved to Tromso, the most northern part of Norway, where her first novel, *Alberta and Jacob*, is set. She first intended to be a painter and attended art school in Oslo. At age twenty-five, she left for Paris, intending to stay for six months, but instead she remained there for fifteen years. Torn between writing and painting, she gave up the latter in 1918 and turned to fiction. (She eventually had an exhibition of her paintings in 1970, when she was ninety years old.) *Alberta and Jacob* was published when she was forty-six years old. It was followed by *Alberta and Freedom* and *Alberta Alone*. Other works include *A Blue Sofa, The Leech, Our Complicated Life*, and several collections of short stories.

Antonio Skármeta was born in Antofagasta, Chile, in 1940. He studied philosophy, literature, and theater directing at the University of Chile and at Columbia University. Until the military coup of Pinochet, he worked in Chile as a professor and journalist. He then went into exile in Berlin, where he wrote four novels and became a film writer and director. He has also translated into Spanish works by the American writers Melville, Fitzgerald, Golding, Mailer, and Kerouac. Skármeta's works include *I Dreamt the Snow Was Burning, Burning Patience, The Insurrection, Chileno!, The Postman,* and *Watch Where the Wolf Is Going.* With the return of democracy to Chile, Skármeta moved to Santiago, where he now lives.

Pramoedya Ananta Toer, Indonesia's major novelist, was born in Blora, a small town on the north coast of Java, in 1925. His father was a teacher and nationalist; his mother was the daughter of a mosque official. Pramoedya was the eldest of nine children. He began his education under his father's tutelage but was a poor student. After finishing his primary education, he took a radio technician's course prior to the outbreak of the Second World War. After the war, he was involved in active resistance against the British and joined the Voice of Free Indonesia in 1946. He was jailed by the Dutch in 1947 and by his own government from 1965 to 1979. Pramoedya's commitment to democratic ideals is reflected in all his works, which are banned in Indonesia. He won international acclaim with his major work, a quartet of novels: *This Earth of Mankind, Child of All Nations, Footsteps,* and *The Fugitive,* which were written in prison. Denied the use of writing materials, he committed his books to memory with the help of his fellow prisoners. His fiction and nonfiction have been translated into sixteen languages. He was the recipient of the PEN American Center Freedom-to-Write Award in 1988.

Xiao Hong (Zhang Naiying) was born in Heilongjiang, Northeast China, in 1911. After enduring a harsh upbringing in a traditional landlord family, she fled an arranged marriage and went to study in Beijing in 1931. She set up house with the poet Xiao Jun, with whom she published a joint collection of short stories. When the Japanese invaded Manchuria in 1933, the two fled to Shanghai, where Xiao Hong was befriended by the famous writer Lu Xun, who helped establish her in the literary world. The story "Hands" was written during this time. Her first novel, *The Field of Life and Death*, written at the age of twenty-three, brought her acclaim. Following the outbreak of war with Japan, Xiao Hong traveled to the interior of China, where she left Xiao Jun and married another writer, Duanmu Hongliang. Her promising literary career was cut short by her death in 1942, at age thirty, of tuberculosis.

ABOUT THE EDITOR

Anne Mazer grew up in a family of writers in upstate New York. She has studied art and French literature, traveled in Europe and Asia, and worked at a variety of jobs. Her children's books range from the bestselling picturebook *The Salamander Room* to middle-grade novels such as *Moose Street*, a Booklist Editor's Choice, and *The Accidental Witch*. She is also known for her young adult short story collection *A Sliver of Glass*, and the *The Oxboy*, an ALA Notable Book. Her anthologies for Persea Books—*America Street*, a finalist for the Hungry Mind Best Young Adult book; *Going Where I'm Coming From*; and *Working Days*, an ALA Best Book for Teens—have been used in classrooms from elementary to college level, and are all New York Public Library Best Books for Teens. Anne Mazer lives in Ithaca, New York, with her two children.